THE SWEET SPELL OF SUCCESS

BETTINA M JOHNSON

Aqua Raven Publishing

The Sweet Spell of Success

ISBN: 978-1-7365176-2-8 (paperback)

Cover art by Stunning Book Covers

CHAPTER 1

"I think I can hit her from here and make it look like an accident."

"Too much blood. And you'll have gunpowder residue on your hand. Considering *you* will be the prime suspect, that isn't a good thing."

"What about a bow and arrow?"

"One shift of the wind and it might go astray and hit—who is that? Abner? You wouldn't want that, despite how much you grumble."

"What's the good in having magic at my disposal if I can't use it to bring down the root of all evil?"

My cousin Andrea chuckled, patting me on the back.

"Lily, as much as you hate Tiffany Clarkston, I doubt she is the root of all evil. Have you not met our great-granny? Adriana is the definition of pure evil—just go look it up in the witch dictionary. Her photo is in there and everything. I think she went to a professional studio to get her headshot done."

I shot a withering look Andrea's way then continued to scrutinize Tiffany Clarkson, "of the Sweet Briar Clarksons," since that is how she constantly introduced herself. At first, I thought she might be related to our new medical examiner, but then I remembered his name was Clark*ston*, and I disabused myself of that notion. I never met any Clarksons and I didn't get around to asking anyone in my family or any friends who they might be. I've recently decided being a dark witch is a good thing but only if it means world domination, death, and destruction with all of my wrath raining down on our newest deputy. Somehow I didn't think the rest of the witches in our town would agree with my certitude. They collectively adored the slut.

Even Lorcan, my fiancé, a label that quickly might be retracted if he continued to drop everything to go, "help the poor girl fix her flat tire," or, "get her pet bunny, Lucifer, back in his pen after he broke free." What did she expect? She named the poor thing Lucifer. He probably has a complex by now—especially since she had his tail dyed hot pink! I kid you not.

"If Abner were two feet to her left, I'd risk the shot," I declared.

"Well, he's not. And I don't have any bail money on me since I treated you to lunch and now I'm tapped until I next hit the bank."

To add insult to injury, Brian Chase, my ex-flame—although we didn't have much of a fire going before we'd parted—had witnessed the bunny roundup and subsequent hot pink, lipstick-covered Lorcan sheepishly returning to his shop after playing hero. I still haven't heard the end of it. And who does Tiffany think she's fooling? Taking the rental house that backs the alley that connects my studio and Lorcan's mechanic shop. Not me! I know what she's up to.

"Did you notice her and Nora coming out of Gloria's

salon the other day? Nora has been skulking around town quite a lot lately, I even saw her walking past your street. She's up to no good as usual! And now Nora and Tiffany are as thick as thieves, which is pure bull. By the time high school was over, those two weren't on speaking terms. I think it's a case of the enemy of my enemy is my friend. Or is that the enemy of my friend? I never can get that straight!" Andrea complained.

"More like the fiancé of my enemy. It doesn't matter what she does with Nora. If Tiffany won't back off and Lorcan doesn't stop running every time she beckons, I don't think I can..."

"Stop! Lily! Don't you dare say the words. You are giving Tiffany power over you with all this negativity. You are better than that! Lorcan loves you. He can't help it if he's a good egg which means he believes the same in everyone he meets—unless they prove him wrong. Right now, Tiffany is playing a game that he is too blind—or kind—to see."

I watched as Tiffany, laughing at something Abner just told her, glanced my way. I scolded myself internally as the urge to jump behind the side of June's Emporium took over. Thankfully, I stopped myself before I could react. She gave me a derisive once over then sniffed, turning back to Abner with a response. He beamed and nodded then went on his way. I couldn't even scold him later for speaking with the enemy—no one felt the least bit of animosity toward the leggy blonde deputy. It's like she put some kind of spell over the entire town.

"I get it. Trust me, I do, cuz. How do you think I feel with that woman sniffing around my brother, Steve, and him acting like a complete and utter asshat at the very mention of her name? It makes me sick."

"It makes me want to slug someone," I replied.

"Quick! Look! Maureen Kennedy is heading our way. She is probably on her way back from lunch. I'll hold her down and you can get in a few jabs before anyone notices."

I looked askance at Andrea, then burst out laughing—something I believe she'd intended to pull me out of my foul mood. Well, it worked. By the time Maureen reached the front entrance of June's Emporium, both Andrea and I were snickering like imbeciles. She gave us a dark look which set us off even more, and we had tears pouring down our faces by the time we'd regained some semblance of control.

"Thanks, Dre. I needed that."

"Don't mention it. Although is it bad that part of me would've really loved to have seen you take me up on my offer?"

"To beat up Maureen or bail me out after I trounced Tiffany?"

"How about both?"

"How about you two dummies stop gossiping about the nonsensical and lend me a hand? We have a huge problem."

Andrea and I jumped at the voice coming from behind us, turning to watch as our great-grandmother, Adriana, strode in our direction before stopping where we stood. She crossed her arms and began tapping her foot impatiently.

"How do you always manage to sneak up on us without our knowing?" I asked.

Adriana chose not to answer, instead grabbing both of our arms and yanking us back toward the alley behind our friend June's store.

"Ow! Stop it, you insane lunatic. Why are you...*oomph*!"

Adriana stopped short causing Andrea to swing around

and smack into me. Then she looked both ways as if she were afraid of being overheard.

"I've no time for your bellyaching, Missy. Didn't you hear me? We have trouble."

"What kind of trouble? Don't tell me you did something to upset the Council. Just because I took over my father's position doesn't mean I am going to let you get away with anything. Despite you being my..."

"Liliana! Would you hush? This is bigger than any stupid Council. We are under attack! Or *will* be," Adriana scolded darkly.

That got my attention, and I clamped my mouth shut and peered at my great-grandmother who looked distracted—not at all like her usually mean and gleeful self.

"What is it now? What has happened?"

"What has happened is I've heard from my Romano relatives in Italy. Something I never thought would happen again in my lifetime. They are sending a delegation to Sweet Briar to meet with us to discuss the coven out west. Apparently, they want us to take action and intend to join us when we do."

I shivered a bit at her words—like a goose just crossed over my grave. Why do I now suppose the proverbial poop was about to hit the fan? A fan on high speed to boot?

❧

WE CONTINUED to the alley behind June's Emporium. June Carter was a family friend and related to my Aunt Iona and Uncle Owen. June is Owen's baby sister. I'd stayed with her in the apartment she'd graciously offered me upon my arrival to Sweet Briar a few months back. Her son, Jake, is one of the first people I met when I'd moved here from upstate New York. This was back before I discovered I was born in Georgia, right here in this town, and had a plethora of relatives in a fifty-mile radius.

The last thing I needed was an Italian delegation showing up in town with a long list of grievances.

The three of us continued to Main Street then turned left and went one block to my street. I lived so close to the town center, I often walked everywhere instead of taking my Jeep. Trudging up the porch steps, I paused to check how the sweetbriar rose bush was faring. It was right up against the house near my back door which led to a mudroom. The shrub was just starting to bloom. Covered in tiny purple buds, it already gave off an intoxicating scent reminiscent of apples. I gave the bush a fond smile then unlocked the door allowing Adriana and Andrea to enter ahead of me then I followed in their wake.

"Adelaide is giving the rose bush her blood offering monthly now, correct?" Adriana asked.

My mother had been doing this ritual yearly, even when fused inside my cat, Wicked. The magic that turned her allowed her to roam free one day a year so she could perform the blood ritual which allowed my dad to remain alive. Lately, she began a campaign of feeding the bush her blood on a monthly basis, even though I didn't think it would matter to my dad. Plus, I hated seeing her slice her palm open allowing a few drops to trickle down and land at the base of the bush—although it did infuse the shrub with enough magic to reach my father. We now knew it worked all these years because we recently came face-to-face—well face-to-computer screen, anyway—with him. He was indeed alive, but not well. He looked sickly and confused as if he wasn't in his right mind.

A prisoner of the woman who destroyed our family twenty-two years ago now, we'd discovered Charlie Sweet had been living with her in the Pacific Northwest all this time. It was shocking, not only because he'd been bound to Deanna Fredricks with dark magic, but that she was behind all of the horrible misdeeds. Especially since my family erroneously thought she'd been murdered by her sister Donna. All this time we'd had it wrong. Donna was under a confound spell which caused her to believe she'd killed Deanna. In reality, Deanna was very much among the living and the supreme mastermind who had fooled many folks, allowing her the freedom to perform all manner of diabolical things.

Her reign of terror was about to come to an end.

"Yes, and I wish she'd stop. She's been doing it all these years. Why cut herself so often now? We know Dad is alive." I followed the two women into my sunporch, and we sat around the table. Wicked was sunning herself on her favorite ledge and didn't even twitch to acknowledge our presence.

"Adelaide is worried about Charlie now that she's seen him with her own eyes. He is skeletal and sickly, Liliana. I am sure she hopes her blood magic will help heal him in some way and counter whatever Deanna is doing to cause him to be so ill." Adriana explained away my mother's obsessive behavior, but I still felt Adelaide's actions were folly.

"Where is Addy, anyway?"

"She's with Aunt Iona and Uncle Owen and will be home in a bit. I'm having them over for dinner tonight." I watched as this news filtered through my great-grandmother's thought process and groaned inwardly when she snapped her fingers in an "aha!" moment.

"Good! This is good! We can call Chiara and tell her to come as well. Liliana, you need to call Jake and Becky. And of course, the Reids need to be here with Lorcan. I will make pasta, so I better get the sauce on."

Adriana stood and rushed into my kitchen where she began rummaging around the cabinets taking out the items she'd need to accomplish this task.

"But ..."

"Look at these cabinets! Don't you believe in organization?" Adriana complained.

"Hang on! I didn't say anything about you joining us. As a matter of fact ..."

"You call this a pot? I'm thinking penne. It goes well with tomato and basil sauce. I usually wait until I have fresh ingredients from my garden, but a quality product from the supermarket will do. I can doctor anything to make it my own. My sauce is delicious," Adriana said as she began pulling items out of my pantry.

"Hold on! Listen. I don't have much ..."

"Just in time! Your eggs are almost out of date. You need to keep a better eye on your expiration dates."

I turned to my cousin to see if she thought Adriana was out of line, but Andrea smartly refrained from engaging in any of the goings-on and was focused on her phone, scrolling through images on a social media site.

"Will you please stop!? Why am I having everyone over? It was just going to be an intimate dinner with the four of us and ..."

"And we need to discuss the arrival of my relatives and what we are going to do about them. I was going to suggest you come to my house, but since Iona and Owen are coming here it makes sense. Now, where is your pasta machine?"

Pasta machine?

CHAPTER 2

Dinner wound up being another massive get-together of friends and relatives. By the time Adriana came around to realizing that not only did I not have a pasta machine, but my cupboards were pretty bare, we wound up putting in an emergency order for Joe Brooks over at his diner. I was now unpacking various goodies out of a huge box Joe had carefully bundled up for our feast.

"Is that stroganoff? I love Joe's stroganoff, it's incredible," Andrea said, while she unpacked another equally stuffed box.

"We have enough food here to feed an army—or this family." I tried not to show how upset I was that Adriana sidelined my plans. My great-grandmother had a habit of running roughshod over everyone and anyone who got in her way.

I was frequently front and center in her assaults and had tread marks on my back to prove it.

"Everyone should be here any minute now, so go ahead and take these to the dining room table," I said.

Everyone being the aforementioned Aunt Iona and Uncle Owen who would bring my mom with them. My Aunt Chiara, Uncle Stephen, and Steve Junior—Andrea's parents and half-brother, would be here as well. I also invited Eileen and Henry Reid, my fiancé's parents. Lorcan was arriving shortly and had informed me he called our friends Jake Carter and Becky Nolan. Jake and Becky are dating, and he was the son of June and Dennis Carter, also invited. My cousin Sophia and her husband Sebastiano were invited but declined as they were preparing for their daughter Fiona's much-anticipated graduation. I think they were grateful the unruly Fiona had made it to the end of her high school years and would be off to college in the fall. She'd been a handful and now they could send her off and hope for the best...and be free of their willful daughter for a time.

"Hurry, hurry, Liliana. Put the food out. No, you want the hot stuff on one side of the buffet and the cold on the other. Where are the rolls?" Adriana began barking out orders causing Andrea and me to jump.

"They are on the kitchen table by the..."

"Do you have wine? All I see is beer. I don't think young ladies should have so much beer in their homes. In my day, one sip of wine would be sufficient."

And when would that be? The 1900s or—*gulp*—the 1800s? I wasn't about to ask.

"I think there is a bottle or two in the pantry by the..."

"No! The napkins go on the other side. You are doing everything incorrectly. Get those wax fruit thingies off the kitchen table before someone mistakes them for real food and breaks a tooth. I mean really! Give me those napkins."

"OK. That's it!" I slapped my hand down on the table making the glassware rattle and one of the shiny fake apples fall out of the bowl and roll onto the floor. "What the heck is wrong with you? No. Forget I asked that—I *already* know what's wrong with you. Why are you so worked up? Are you off your meds again?" I had to forcibly stop Adriana from yanking the napkins out of Andrea's hands. She was now cowering in the corner of my dining room waiting for my great-grandmother to smite me for challenging her actions.

"Give me back those napkins."

"No. Answer the question, old lady."

"Give them back, now, Liliana."

"No. Not until you tell me what's wrong."

"This is my final warning!"

"Or what? Are you going to..."

Zap!

"Jeebers!"

"Oh, my goodness! Granny! What did you do?" cried Andrea.

What she did was hit me with the vilest, most horribly salacious dark magic ever known to humankind...or witchkind, rather.

"What happened to Lily's clothing? She's naked!"

And that's when all my guests arrived. Most of them could bear witness to me streaking across the living room, through the foyer, and up the stairs but not before slamming into Pandora who materialized out of thin air.

"Whoa! I'm gone a week and that's when you start the orgy?" Pandora asked with a giggle.

"Move!" I flew up the stairs and didn't stop running until I reached my room, where I slammed the door, locking it behind me. That's when it dawned on me all I had to do was snap *my* fingers to be fully clothed once more.

I am going to kill that old witch if it's the last thing I do.

❧

Any time you feel like having me over for a dinner show again, I'm willing," said Steve. "I am still trying to figure out if you are supposed to be Lady Godiva or you are in a revival of Oh! Calcutta!" He laughed then ducked when I threw my roll at his head.

"Very funny. Ha, ha," I replied, looking morose.

"Chin up, Lily. At least you have a killer body. I'd walk around naked all day if I looked like you." I know Andrea meant well, but all that managed to do was make my blush deepen. I groaned and put my head down on the table.

"Poor Abner. Did you see his face? He was just outside that window there when Lily ran by. I've never seen a man drop a pipe out of his mouth and manage to catch the mulch on fire. We're lucky the house didn't go up it spread so quickly!" Andrea continued.

"Abner? Forget him. Did you hear what Adriana said? Lily was trying to escape so fast she didn't register Edith gliding toward her from the living room and ran straight through her! Adriana said Edith may never get over the shock of that full-frontal attack!" Jake chuckled.

I sat up giving him my most menacing look which set everyone off laughing even harder.

"I'm for all naked all the time. Who's with me?" Pandora piped up.

I snapped my fingers in her direction and she settled down. You have to treat her like a disobedient puppy or she gets ideas. It didn't stop Steve from opening his mouth to reply, so I snapped my fingers in his direction as well. Jake and Lorcan just appeared a bit dazed and came out of whatever daydreams they'd been having, so I killed two birds with one stone. Having everyone focused and off the subject of my naked antics, I steered the conversation to what was bugging Adriana, and we got down to business.

Steve was trying to get Pandora's attention, but she was pointedly ignoring him.

I didn't have the time right now to confront Pandora—regarding Steve *and* her abrupt reappearance—even though that was the only thing on my mind. Adriana commanded all my attention and that of everyone present.

"Granny was agitated all throughout dinner. What is so bad with the relatives coming from Italy that has her this worked up?"

June turned from her conversation with Eileen Reid and responded. "The Romanos have never left Rome with the exception of the few that went rogue. I don't think Adriana has seen any of them in years. Decades even," she informed us. "That must be the cause of your grandmother's disquiet."

Disquiet? Disorder is more like it. Unhinged even.

"When are they arriving anyway?" I asked.

"I think sometime in the next two weeks. Although I couldn't get a straight answer out of any of them when I called yesterday," Chiara said. My aunt was borderline psychotic herself over the upcoming visit, although she hid it better than Adriana.

We were mostly finished with our meal and had dessert to look forward to, so I stood to go make the coffee and put the kettle on for those who preferred tea. Joe had outdone himself and we were stuffed on not only the beef stroganoff, but chicken marsala, eggplant rollatini, sausage with peppers, and penne with vodka sauce. The sides were plentiful, and everyone had seconds, if not thirds.

"Becky, could you help gather up these plates so I can tackle the coffee? Jake, you can help please."

"Of course!" Jake stood, rushing over to Becky's chair

and held it while she stood. Then they began clearing the dishes. Andrea and Lorcan rose to help as well. I was halfway to the kitchen when a loud explosion shattered the normalcy of the moment. Glass went in every direction, and my guests threw themselves down and out of the way flinging their arms up to protect themselves from the deadly missiles.

It sounded like a bomb going off or a train collision.

When the dust settled, I couldn't believe what I was seeing.

Where Abner had been standing earlier tending to my mulch which he'd set on fire in his shock at my bare state, a large Lincoln Town Car now existed, having come to rest in the opening that used to be my huge picture window. Sitting behind the wheel blinking in confusion was my great-grandfather, Antonio Dolce.

He gave us a little wave.

Then all hell broke loose.

CHAPTER 3

"Get him out of that car! Oh goodness is he injured?" screeched Adriana. Uncle Owen reached the car first and gently pulled the old man out after first ascertaining he didn't have any severe injuries. That didn't stop my Aunt Chiara from immediately calling Shirley Jones, our EMT, to check him over. Some of the men were about to move the car but Eileen stopped them knowing the insurance would need to see the mess, so instead, they began snapping photos.

Shirley was now working on Antonio in my den even though he kept insisting nothing hurt and he was perfectly fine. He didn't even have one scratch.

"I can't believe no one was hurt. Not even Antonio!" Aunt Chiara cried.

"I can't believe no one passed out. That has to be a first in this family. Usually, we have one thing go down and we're mopping up the place with the bodies of those overcome with shock and awe."

The only shock and awe present was on the face of the

claims adjuster who was even now looking over the damage to my dining room.

"We do not pass out over every little thing!" grumbled Aunt Iona. She was touchy when the subject came up because she still wasn't over her little episode a few weeks back when we'd left her passed out on my side porch while we had to ignore her and retrieve Adelaide from her similar state in my backyard. Both of them went down like boulders tossed in a swimming pool.

I shouldn't jest because until recently, I hit the deck every time one dramatic event happened after another...and in this family, the frequency of chaotic incidents meant I saw the back of my eyelids more than a coma patient. Thankfully, I learned how to control my siren magic rushing up simultaneously with my witch magic which caused me to short circuit and often pass out. Now I didn't even flinch when something traumatic occurred.

Seriously.

I don't think I blinked even once just now and I'm the one with a Lincoln doubling as a window planter box. I barely even registered a reaction and that worries me. Shouldn't I be more concerned that my great-grandfather could have injured himself or others? A scream? Ducking to the ground? Nothing. I continued walking to the kitchen like I didn't have a care in the world and put on that pot of coffee.

What?

You know we'd still have some...we have pastries!

It took an hour to clear up the mess and for Lorcan, Jake, and Steve to nail plywood over the window opening with their dads giving advice on how to properly achieve this task. We waited for the adjuster to leave and made the shattered glass slivers disappear with magic, but I'd still have to order a new window. I was mildly disappointed none of those present could snap their fingers and have a new one installed in seconds. We witch folk were good, but we weren't *that* good.

"He's all done," proclaimed Shirley, "I didn't need to bandage him or anything.

"It's a miracle," said Aunt Chiara. Now that she knew her grandfather was fine, Chiara turned toward him with a frown and began scolding his reckless behavior.

"What did you think you were doing? You haven't driven in years! Do you even have a license anymore, Grandfather? You could have been injured...or worse! *And* you could have harmed someone else."

I looked at Andrea and the same thought passed between us. *Had he injured anyone along the way?* We'd have to call the sheriff and report this incident just in case. Although I didn't want my great-grandpa in trouble, we might have a few injured residents from here to the aged Victorian mansion Antonio and Adriana called home. Or maybe I'd send someone to check first. Glancing at Shirley as she repacked her medical bag, I think I knew who that would be. I noticed the dark circles under Shirley's eyes and her usually jovial self was rather subdued. I wondered if what had been bothering her a few weeks back was still a concern, and I knew I'd have to have a chat with her to answer that question—and offer my help if she needed me.

Right now, we had the pressing matter of Antonio to deal with. Once we had Shirley on her way with the promise to inform us if she found any dead or dying citizens of Sweet Briar, we turned our attention to the contrite Antonio, who was sipping an espresso, trying to look nonchalant.

"OK, old man. Start talking! What gives?" I asked.

"Geeve? I no geeve anything. I drive. Ma she no go where I ask!" he replied.

"But why did you have to go anywhere, Grandfather? Any one of us would have come for you. Or wait a minute," exclaimed Andrea, "Where is Keisha? Shouldn't she have been with you?"

"Is why I come. Keisha vai a prendere la pizza. But she no come back," said Antonio.

Keisha went out for pizza? That doesn't make sense, not when she could have ordered one in.

"Did she tell you she was leaving to get pizza, or did she say something else?" I asked.

"She say, 'you wait I go get la pizza.' An I wait. Then I wait more, ma no Keisha. An I think ma maybe she is malato o ferito...or someone he take! So I come." Antonio looked so worried that none of us felt like continuing our scolding. Andrea sat by his side and gave him a hug. Adriana was on her husband's other side but now stood up and began to pace.

"Let me call her. I hope she didn't fall ill or become injured, but let's not jump to conclusions on her being abducted just yet. She has a cell, and this one has his as well," she jerked her thumb at Antonio, "but can never remember how to answer it—or make a call." Pulling out her phone she called our friend and Antonio's nurse. It went to voice mail.

"I'm calling the sheriff."

"Maybe we should call Susanne or Doc Holcomb?" Andrea suggested and began itching her elbow in a nervous habit.

"I'm on it," said Aunt Iona. She went into the kitchen to make the call and get the pastries out.

What? I told you they were high on our list. Although I didn't have much of an appetite what with Keisha missing and all. Much.

"Huh," Iona said when she returned a few moments

later and she disconnected the call with the sheriff. She sat across from my great-grandfather with a frown on her face and rubbed the back of her neck. We were all standing around waiting for her to explain her reaction to whatever Sheriff Buford said to her, but she was taking her sweet time acknowledging the eager faces staring her way.

Chiara finally had enough. "Well? What did Glen say?"

Iona startled and glanced around the room as if she'd just noticed us for the first time.

"Glen said he didn't have anyone he could spare right now and to do a search for Keisha ourselves. It seems Sheila called him a bit ago frantic that Gordy had gone missing. His truck was found parked and running in the back of the laundromat and he hadn't collected the garbage yet. Then old Mrs. Ramirez called, frantic over the fact Martha had up and disappeared from the library. Martha is the only one who locks up but was nowhere on the property. Her car is still there, her handbag as well. It looks like she's been abducted! But what's even worse? The hospital called. It seems Rowena escaped from the mental facility and is nowhere to be found. She's missing and at large!"

The doorbell rang, startling everyone, and as I rushed to see who was at the front door, I had a premonition hit me that had me suspecting I would not like who I'd find on the other side.

"Miss Sweet. I'm so sorry to disturb you, and it looks as if you've already had your fair share of disturbances around here—oh, you have a hole in your wall!"

Tiffany Clarkson stood simpering, her fake concern on full display and her eyes sparkling with unbridled glee at my discomfort. I knew I wouldn't like who I found when I opened my front door—no one uses it, ever! I should have listened to my intuition. At least it wasn't the tilty-head Rowena holding a bloody knife—or worse—wielding powerful magic. I returned Tiffany's sneer by baring my teeth and responded with my own banalities.

"How unexpected. What can I do for you, Miss Clarkson?"

"Officer Clarkson," she subtly corrected me.

"Hey, Tiffany. What's up?" Lorcan came up behind me and put his arm around my shoulders. I watched in satisfaction as Tiffany frowned slightly before catching herself then gave Lorcan a bright smile.

"Well, hello there, neighbor. Fancy meeting you here! You used to loathe drama of any kind, so I'm surprised you haven't run to the hills yet seeing as how much keeps popping up in current company."

I hate her.

I had visions of brutality and vindictive behavior coursing through my mind and almost smiled when a particularly nasty thought took hold. However, I checked myself in time, swallowing the comment that came unbidden and forcefully, then composed my face into one of abject ennui. I gave Tiffany a lazy blink and stifled a yawn for her benefit.

She squinted slightly then focused on Lorcan once more. "I stopped by because we've had some complaints from neighbors about the commotion. A few said the racket was at decibels beyond what they could take another moment, but then I heard over the scanner that a great negligence occurred where this family allowed a relative with dementia to get behind the wheel of a vehicle. Pity, that."

"My husband does not have dementia. He became slightly confused and worried about his nurse which caused him to act against his better judgment." Adriana crept up behind us and popped around the side of me to confront the snide deputy. "Furthermore, he doesn't comprehend how to use his cell phone—the language barrier and modern-day contraption give him difficulty—but he's hardly suffering from dementia," she sniffed.

"Mmhmm...same thing perhaps." Tiffany dismissed my great-grandmother and continued her little diatribe not realizing how close to annihilation she was getting. Even Lorcan was picking up on Adriana's mood shift and my willing her to act upon it.

"Anyway, I stopped in to inform you of the very many complaints, well—not *you,* Lorcan—this family, since I felt it my duty that they understand that repeated and escalating incidents such as this could alienate them from the community and lead to citations or worse. Not that I'd enjoy having to go that far as to write them up for disturbing the peace or anything."

"Oh, I think you'd like nothing better, missy. I think you'd like it very much if I'd do something to disturb the peace right now. And if you don't get off my great-granddaughter's porch and skedaddle in that overblown excuse of an SUV that compensates for your lack of a third leg which causes you to become an overaggressive skank, you will find out just how much disturbing of the peace I will rain down upon this town. Now leave." Adriana crackled her knuckles then took a step forward.

Not to be outdone by my diminutive granny, Tiffany flashed a condescending smile and began speaking slowly and loudly as if she were dealing with a hard of hearing senile old lady. "Ms. Dolce, aren't you just a sweet old thing? Don't you worry none, hon. I won't be arresting your husband this time. He couldn't help himself and all—what with his advanced state. Don't you fret none." Turning to Lorcan once more, Tiffany rested her hand on his arm and gave it a firm squeeze. "I will be running along now, sweetie. I will see you tomorrow. Oh! Unless you happen to catch me forgetting my window blinds open again! And me coming out of the shower and all—such a silly thing I can be at times! OK, folks. You mind your elderly and keep the noise level and drama at a low keel, hear?"

And with that, Tiffany turned on a stiletto heel and sashayed back to her vehicle with a toss of her golden locks and a hand firmly on her holster.

The fool didn't realize that if we wanted her eliminated, no gun could stop us.

Slamming the door in her wake, I faced Adriana and a look passed between us before she addressed everyone at large in a commanding voice.

"We don't have time for middle-grade hijinks. I will get to that tramp when this is over with. Right now, we have a kidnapping spree to solve and a menace to grind to dust." Turning to Lorcan, Adriana said in a low voice, "And if I ever catch you staring into that hussy's open window, I know who I will blame for distracting me from my task, and just *what* I will be turning into dust to compensate for lost time."

Lorcan blanched. Well, then, maybe that bit of guidance made it into my fiancé's thick skull. I know I gulped!

CHAPTER 4

I cleared everyone out of my house, including a protesting Lorcan, and got down to the business I had put off with the craziness of the day—but not for lack of interest. If anything, this was the only thing I cared about right now, even more so than the missing residents and the Tiffany situation.

"How did you do what you did and what did you find out while you were there?"

Confronting Pandora and her abrupt return had been consuming me. I wanted to know what she'd found out about my dad. I wanted to understand her intentions and why and how she managed to get clear across the nation and managed to be precisely where Deanna Fredricks was holding my father prisoner. How could she have managed this? And more importantly, could she take me to him?

"I missed you too, sugar."

"Cut the crap, Dorie. When did you get back?"

"I returned the moment you slammed into me in your delightfully unclothed condition," she said. "You may want to consider keeping that your permanent look—it certainly is one way of battling Tiffany Clarkson of the Sweet Briar Clarksons."

Pandora ended her statement in a singsong voice, eerily mimicking the wretched deputy and her standard mode of introduction.

"I don't know why you are being so sour with me. I thought I did good, crossing an entire country and managing to land a mere half-mile from where the renegade witches are camping out. Of course, I had to hike through the woods and sneak into their compound without drawing attention to myself. But when I realized there was no way anyone would overlook me in all my magnificence, I decided to put on a glamour that I made sure would only affect that bunch of unwashed heathens."

I scrunched my face into a prune-like mien and gazed at my demon acquaintance with scrutiny. I did not understand the motivations and machinations of this chick. Not one bit. I knew my great-grandmother and mom both trusted Pandora, but I still hadn't decided if I did. But right now, she had a leg up since she'd been front and center in the enemy camp, so to speak.

"Did you speak with my dad? Is he...does he remember us?" I asked and hated how fragile I sounded.

Dorie's face immediately softened, and she gave me an understanding look. "Charlie is a mess. I delved deeply into his mind, and I didn't find much I recognized. It seems there is a trace of the man, boy really, I knew, but so much is utter chaos. I think he is lost to..."

"No! I refuse to believe he is lost to us. No way."

"Lily! I wasn't going to say that!" Pandora scolded. "I was trying to say I think he is lost to his own dark thoughts—lost in his own mind. It will take time to remove the years of damage then lead him out of that tangled web of lies and magical mind alterations and get him to a place where he can heal. He's in there, Lily. But he is perplexed—his thoughts aimlessly wandering through a web of false memories."

"Take me to him."

"I can't."

"Don't feed me that line of BS, Dorie. I saw you with my own eyes. If you can go there, so can I. Take me there. Now!"

Pandora's eyes opened wide in alarm at my vehemence.

"Whoa, sugar. Hold on a second. You've got the wrong idea about..."

"Take me to my father now or leave my home. I don't need your help...not your kind. Not when you could have taken me to him all this time and didn't bother sharing that little tidbit with any of us. I don't trust you. I don't know you. And I don't care to get to know you any better when you are obviously perfectly OK with deceiving me and my family."

Pandora's mouth dropped open during my diatribe, but she closed it now with a snap of her teeth.

She squinted and it was my turn to pause in alarm at the immediate change in her demeanor—the temperature in the room dropped and Pandora morphed into something frightening and menacing in an instant. He outward appearance did not change, other than looking royally pissed, but her eyes began to glow an unearthly red with flames flickering deep in their depths.

"Listen, sweet stuff. Let me make something perfectly clear. I am here because I care about both of your parents. I am here because I owe Jessica. Her life was cut short, and she never got to live the one she dreamed about. I'm here because I respect Adriana and Antonio and hate to see the suffering they have gone through because their familial angst and ancestry is so messed up those two never had a chance to live without looking over their shoulders for the next attack. Those two kids broke the mold and decided to choose the path of good over the easier path of evil, and someone like me? We tend to admire the strength it takes to shun hereditary traits and forge a new destiny." Pandora slammed my chair back in place as she stood to face me.

"I was there when Marcus Romano lost his beloved Amelia to poison, their newborn baby, Luigi, crying in the background for a mother he would never meet. I was there when Luigi fell in love with Elisabetta and they had their only child, Adriana—your great-grandmother. I watched her grow from an enchanting little girl into a formidable dark witch. I watched her fall in love with Antonio and witnessed their incredibly romantic courtship which led to marriage and the birth of Antonio, Jr. I was there when they mourned his loss in a car accident that took him and his bride." Dorie closed the distance between us and came nose to nose with me, but I didn't move back or flinch as she spat each word in my direction.

"I was there when little Charlie cried himself to sleep missing his parents who would never return from their grand tour of the Far East. I was there when he first met Jessica and they became fast friends even though her annoying little sister was always tagging along with them everywhere they went. I was there when Charlie noticed Adelaide, not as that annoying sibling trying to keep up with big sister Jessica, but as an enchanting creature, he was quickly losing his heart to. I was there when they fell deeply in love and planned to run off to marry in secret. I was there when you were born." Here she paused and Pandora's voice dropped into a caustic whisper, "and despite what you just said, you *do* know me well, Lily Sweet. I was there every night of your young life—my tales were the last words you heard before you dropped off to sleep at night. So, save me your attitude and threats. And by all means, continue to not trust me. It's no skin off my back."

"Tales? Your tales lulled me to sleep?" It was the only thing I could manage to squeak out after absorbing all I'd just heard—especially since the reality of just how ancient a being Pandora is became apparent in her recalling her ties to my family. "But why? Why are you so invested in my family? You act as if we...no. Oh, my gosh. Are we? Does this mean...Dorie! Are we related?"

"Kissing kin."

How do you like that? It's not enough that I can pick up a rock and randomly throw it in this town and I will assuredly hit a long-lost relation. But now I find out I am related to a siren *and* a demon—not to mention the Fredricks sisters who have been trying to kill me and destroy my family to boot. What an incestuous bunch of paranormals we are!

"Please just tell me I am in no way related to Lorcan, and I'm good."

"I think you're safe, sugar. Well, as long as we can keep ol' Tiffany out of his pants."

"May she be swallowed in a pit of venomous vipers," I added.

"Hey, I can make that happen. No sweat."

Maybe Dorie isn't as bad as I made her out to be after all.

CHAPTER 5

"In and among all this new drama, the Council voted and approved your taking over your father's position, Lily," my Aunt Chiara informed me the next day. "However, you will not be in any lead position despite your wishes and what you so eloquently stated a few weeks back. I'm sorry, but the bylaws state you had to be raised among the town of Sweet Briar and the Southeastern region to hold higher office. I'm not saying you will never be an Elder, but you have a few years to go and experience to garner before that will happen."

This news didn't surprise me—annoy yes—but not shocking news in light of the fact I hadn't grown up here or even knew I was a witch until I returned last year.

"I get to vote though, right? I have a say in the goings-on and can voice my opinions?" I asked.

"But, of course."

Well, there was that at least.

The hammering from the new window being installed caused me and my aunt to move from our current position in the dining room to the den where the noise was still grating, but a tad less so. Wicked was sitting on the mantle glaring at the banging sounds coming from Horatio "Bud" Buchannon, my contractor. He'd done all of the work when I decided to renovate and patch up my family home a few months back. His wife, Petunia was handing him nails and they both gave us a little wave as we moved to the den. I think Wicked was afraid the noise and workers would be returning once more to disturb her slumber and cause her no end of agitation.

"Don't worry, furball. Bud will only be here another hour or so and then he will come back tomorrow to patch and paint. Then he'll be all done, and you will have peace once more."

"Meroo?"

"Yes. It's true." I replied.

What? I could tell what Wicked had asked. It was obvious!

She relaxed and jumped down onto the chair beside the fireplace and began to wash. The calm was short-lived however because Petunia chose that moment to barge into the room with Adriana hot on her heels, shattering the peace.

"Did you hear the news?" Petunia asked.

"News?"

"Harley Jacobs' parents are missing!"

Petunia informed us of this disturbing news with a salacious look in her eyes that soured me on the gossipy woman. I mean, I knew she was the ringleader and Queen of All Gossip in this town, but spreading news was one thing—enjoying the misfortune of others is where I drew the line in being understanding about this little bad habit.

"Petunia Buchannon! You should be ashamed of yourself. Tamp down that excitement and show some concern!

I thought Mary Lee was your good friend. You look positively giddy over the news!" Aunt Chiara chided her.

Petunia had the grace to look abashed at being called out for her tactlessness.

"Of course, she's my friend. So is Nathan. I've known the Jacobs all my life!"

"We must get to the bottom of these disappearances! This is getting out of hand—beyond that point, as a matter of fact. This is an epidemic!" Adriana proclaimed.

"I already know what is behind all these disappearances—well, who anyway." Pandora came strolling into the room looking like the cat that caught the canary. "I would have delved a bit deeper into all I learned while away, but the distractions of yesterday sort of made me decide to wait until I could command your attention—without having to fight constant interruption."

Adriana gave Dorie a once over then crossed her arms. "Go ahead. I'm listening."

"Someone from Camp Fredricks is here scouting out the enemy—us—and decided to mess with our heads by kidnapping the residents, some of whom we hold near and dear. Actually, all of them, we consider all of them good friends. Well, *you* do anyway. I don't know many of them yet." Pandora explained.

Petunia stared mouth agape at the visage that was one Pandora, crossroads demon. I almost forgot she wasn't a paranormal herself but a trusted human. Trusted human or not, Pandora was a sight to behold today. I don't know where she conjured up her outfit, but it looked like something you'd totally expect a crossroads demon to be wearing. One on a mission of destruction, that is. Leather thigh-high boots, *barely-there* tight skirt, a demonic bustier of some sort with straps and rings of grommets, open-fingered lace gloves, and her hair done up in an elaborate do. All she needed was a whip, and she'd look like a Madonna wannabe reject from the '80s.

Even *my* mouth was open.

Petunia dropped her purse and Dorie rushed over to retrieve it. Handing it back to the flustered woman, Pandora continued her observations.

"I think we might be able to track this interloper, but we need some help from the blood-sucking crew."

I glanced at Petunia not knowing how much we could say in front of her.

"Should we call Mortimer?" Chiara asked, saving me from causing a faux pas at the last minute because I would have said "vampire" out loud.

"Morty would certainly be an asset," Dorie stated. "After all, a vampire's nose is ten times better than anything else in this world—or out of it, even a demon's!"

I waited for the thud, closing my eyes tightly, but it never came. Opening them a crack to peer at Petunia, I noticed her pale state. She obviously had quite the constitution because she hadn't fainted like I assumed. This was getting positively habit-forming! What would we ever do without the constant vapors to distract us from charging headfirst into the next crisis?

"We don't need Morty. I have something better in mind. I'm going to conjure up a couple of hellhounds," proclaimed Adriana.

Thud!

That's more like it. Turning just in time to see Petunia crash to the ground—out cold—it occurred to me just what my great-grandmother had said. But I was too distracted by Pandora who'd leaned over to help Chiara lift the prone Petunia. Dorie failed to remember a certain item of clothing and it was glaringly obvious in her position that she was missing them.

"Dorie! You aren't wearing any underwear!" I shouted.

"Oopsie!" she replied.

With that diversion addressed, my mind returned to the elephant in the room.

Hellhounds?

"Is anyone going to explain what the heck hellhounds are, or am I going to have to wait to find out?" I asked.

"You will find out soon enough, kiddo." Adriana cackled.

"Oh, great. I can't wait for this one," I said.

"Mreow!" Wicked growled from her perch on the armchair.

Indeed. My sentiments exactly, furball.

"AND JUST WHAT ARE HELLHOUNDS AGAIN?"

Despite my asking this very question ten minutes ago, Adriana failed to enlighten me. Pandora was busy on her cell phone to Hades—well, who else could she be calling on that contraption?

Chiara had hustled a flustered Petunia out and into the long-suffering arms of her spouse, Bud. He'd send me the bill were his parting words and I couldn't blame him for rushing away from us as fast as his old Chevy truck could take him—Petunia texting away, assuredly informing the gossip mill of her latest and greatest.

Adriana was sitting at my kitchen table sipping an espresso like she didn't have a care in the world.

"Stop fretting. Max and Rex are the sweetest pooches I've ever come across. They are excellent scent hounds."

"But from hell," I grumbled.

"They are the best kind."

"You can't be serious. This is a joke, right?"

Peering at me like I'd lost all of my marbles, Adriana just shrugged then said, "Sure, OK."

"No. Don't just say that because you think it's what I need to hear."

"OK, then no."

"Not a joke?"

"No, then *no*, I'm not serious."

"So, it *is* a joke!"

"Sure."

Argh!

"Stop saying that! Just tell me the truth!" I yelled while pulling at my hair.

"Liliana. What do you want me to say? Hellhounds are just that. Hounds from hell. They are the best scenters. Nothing can escape detection if they are on your trail. Nothing. They make the Sentinels look like amateurs."

"And you have these beasts at your disposal?" I asked in wonder.

"Well, no. But I know someone who does."

Uh, oh. Why does that make me want to go hide in my bedroom and not come out for a year or two?

There was a brief knock on the back door and Lorcan came in with Jake on his heels. He crossed the room and gave me a tight hug then turned to my great-grandmother.

"I searched all over the woods by Nichols Pond. I haven't found him yet, but Jake and I are confident we'll do so before the end of the day. He is a creature of habit after all."

"Who?" I asked, although I already suspected I knew who Lorcan was referring to.

"Old Frank. He has two hellhounds he keeps hidden away at his cabin, only he wasn't there when we stopped by just now. So, we wandered the woods around Nichols Pond but stopped when we realized he must be somewhere else today. He's not hard to find...not with the pack of dogs he keeps as companions following him everywhere he goes. As a matter of fact..."

Lorcan didn't get to finish his thought when his phone began to ring with urgency even I could feel.

"Reid, here."

"Lorcan! My goodness. Come quick! There is a man at the fairgrounds with a pack of wild dogs and they are chasing some unseen entity and scaring the tourists!" The voice of our sheriff, Glen Buford came across loud and clear—and in a panic.

"I'll be right there!" Lorcan disconnected and turned to me. "You better come with me, Lily. I think I know who Frank is chasing!"

"Who?" I asked, not getting what Lorcan was asking of me.

"Frank must be going after his older brother, Old Greg. The ghost who haunted the girls' bathrooms. Well, it isn't a gymnasium and administration center any longer. It's our new auction house. So, Old Greg must be up to some kind of new hijinks to rile Frank up so!"

Why is my life so odd on any given day?

Didn't I deserve a break?

Don't answer that.

CHAPTER 6

I could not believe the scene playing out in front of me. Part of me accepted that a grizzled mountain man, hopped up on his own moonshine, chasing his pack of shaggy dogs of all shapes and sizes around the fairgrounds, hollering at thin air would in and of itself be unusual. The other part of me, the one that didn't want to accept I could see and hear ghosts looked on in incredulity.

Not only was Old Greg there, keeping just out of reach of the dog pack and his brother, Edith had somehow decided to throw her lot in with Frank—who I was surprised to realize could see *and* hear her. And the two of them were weaving in and out of the throngs of panicked tourists trying to nab the taunting Greg. Well, Frank was weaving, Edith went directly through unsuspecting visitors with abandon.

The only dog not slobbering and snapping at the ghostly Greg—giving me pause when it was obvious even the dogs could track the ghost—was Rusty. He of the "swallowed the prison key" fame when Adriana and my friends and I had our ill-fated attempt to gain access to the lower level of the prison. It was our introduction to Mortimer and would hardly be a day I'd forget any time soon.

Rusty spied us and came loping over, tongue lolling and tail making its slow back and forth wag. He sat and promptly offered me his paw. I shook it then stared at him a moment before speaking. "Do you think you could tell Frank to stop chasing Old Greg and talk with us a moment?"

What? Rusty was a highly intelligent mutt. He didn't even hesitate a second but snorted, turned tail, and ran over to Frank. One loud bark was all it took to distract his master and lead him our way—the chase to capture Greg paused for the moment.

Frank looked displeased but acquiesced, hightailing it in our direction with his pack following. The only one who didn't stop the hunt was Edith. Old Greg and Edith looked like schoolkids playing tag, but at least the tourists couldn't see the goings-on, so for the moment at least, the chaos had ended.

"Frank." Lorcan greeted the old moonshiner.

Frank just gave a curt nod. Old Frank didn't say much although he did throw a shy smile in my direction. Then I watched as his eyes widened when he took in Pandora and her skimpy outfit. He gave her the once over—twice—then one more time for good measure and shook his head in confusion. The dogs' hackles rose, and they backed away from her causing Dorie to pout. I found that strange because Wicked seemed to adore Pandora and oh, wait, hellcat. Got it.

"What's up man? Greg doing something that needs you to scare our bread and butter tourists from the town?" Jake asked.

"My brother is up to no good."

"Elaborate, Frank. We need more here. The sheriff is on the other side of the park trying to calm down a church delegation from Cordelia. They are convinced you were speaking in tongues and possessed the dogs into attacking the masses. Even though any moron could see your pack is well-behaved—well usually, anyway." Lorcan added.

"Greg's been dead for decades. He liked his lot in the girls' gymnasium. You moved it. Now he's upset." Frank shrugged as if that explained everything.

"But it's not like he can do anything to harm the tourists or cause trouble right?" I asked then wondered just how *old,* Old Greg could be since I remembered something Adriana told me about when he roamed the earth in a corporeal state. Wait a minute. That meant Frank and Abner must be ancient, as well! Just how ancient were the three brothers anyway? You could never tell with witches!

"Greg's a tricky one. Learnt how to transfer his energy. Look there!" Frank pointed off into the distance and we watched in amazement as Greg ran past a tourist couple and pinched the woman's derriere as he did, causing the poor woman to shriek. She then turned and slapped a hapless Dev Patel, the veterinary assistant, who was innocently standing behind her watching us. Or watching Frank's dog pack anyway. The man was dedicated to canines, felines, and the rest of the *ines*, as he should be. Poor Dev yelped then blanched when the woman's husband got in his face.

"I'm on it." Jake took off to defuse the situation, and I turned back to Frank with a grimace of understanding.

"What can we do to make Greg stop and go away? I mean, *can* we make him stop and leave?" I asked.

"Can't. Greg does what Greg wants to do. Always was a pain in the ass." Frank sighed then scratched his head.

"Wait a minute. They didn't close the high school. They just moved the facilities across the park and next to the middle school. Why don't we show Greg where the, um...how about we tell him the gymnasium and locker rooms are across the way? Won't that work?" Lorcan suggested and gave me an apologetic look because I was well aware the only reason Old Greg has hung around instead of going off to his great reward was the girls' showers and his Peeping Tom tendencies. Or in this case, Peeping Greg.

Yuck.

"Might could." Frank responded.

"Then again, it might not."

I spun quickly and found Abner standing practically on my heels as he stood there pulling on his lower lip.

I didn't even bother yelling at him. I mean really, what's the point?

"Where did you come from?" I asked instead.

Abner looked at me like he didn't understand my question then shrugged.

"Greg won't never leave unless someone forces him to. Not sure why he wants to hang around here—nekked girls or no."

"Hang on a minute," Pandora muttered then took a few steps toward the fairgrounds. She stood contemplating the scene with her head tilted to one side, hands on hips. "I don't believe this."

Dorie put her fingers in her mouth and blew out a shockingly loud whistle. Everyone on the fairground froze and turned—including Edith and Old Greg. The former blanched whiter than the purest snow, eyes wide and head reared back. The momentary distraction allowed one small unidentifiable wiry mutt of Frank's to land a bite on Old

Greg's behind. The dog's teeth clamped shut with a snap since he couldn't really bite the ghost.

"Get your scrawny butt over here, old man! You slipped out of my grasp twenty-four years ago and I'm not about to lose you again this time around!"

Before I knew what happened, Dorie conjured some kind of arcane magic and hurled it at the hapless Old Greg who was scrambling every which way trying to outmaneuver it. Of course, she did this in full sight of humans, both tourists and the residents of Sweet Briar, and the chaos that ensued was the stuff of legends. This madness was at such a frenzied pitch, that I almost didn't hear my great-grandmother shouting from somewhere to my left. However, I caught sight of her before utter silence reigned, and my astonishment tripled.

Adriana had performed some kind of potent magic of her own because the entire world froze. Seriously. Every single non-magical person was frozen in place like a bizarre mannequin. This left a few of us of the paranormal persuasion staring agog at a shrieking Old Greg, who everyone could now see since Dorie had placed a glorified magical net around him and was dragging him, kicking and screaming, in her direction.

"I ain't goin'! You can't make me! I was only kidding. I never meant what I said!" The whites of Greg's eyes were pronounced since he had them open so wide they appeared stretched to the breaking point.

"Oh, toots. That's what they all say when I come to collect on a bargain. You gave up your soul to me and now it's time to pay the piper!" Pandora was concentrating hard, and the tip of her tongue poked out of her mouth as she maneuvered the struggling ghost to come to rest directly in front of her.

"Now, that's better," she purred. "Howdy, Greg. It's been a while. Ready for your eternal reward?"

I'd be more concerned about Old Greg's fate if Dorie hadn't previously informed me the souls she collected could do a sort of work release and retain their essence after a time. She didn't tell me just how long a stretch in hell—or wherever it was they'd be heading—would be, but that was Old Greg's problem for having made a deal with the crossroads demon in the first place. In my pity for the poor ghost, I almost blurted out that tidbit, but one warning glare from Pandora had me clamping my mouth shut tight.

I watched as she bent forward and waved her hands over the ground, opening up a large hole. She dangled the frightened Greg over the opening then squinted at him before continuing her chastising. "You are getting off easy because we have more pressing matters than an uncooperative old ghost to keep us distracted. Say hi to Guy for me." And with those last words, Dorie dropped a screaming Greg into the hole where he floated down, down, down until we could see him no longer. Dorie remained peering over the edge, hands on her ankles with me beside her until I heard an intake of breath from behind us.

Turning, I found a human child, a boy, holding a candied apple, the sticky remnants of which lined his lips. He was staring at Dorie's bare behind—her lack of underwear obvious to anyone and everyone. Well, it would have been if they weren't frozen. I guessed Adriana must have missed him when she let out her colossal spell.

"Golly!" stated the boy.

"Dorie!" I shouted in frustration.

Standing up and straightening her skirt, Pandora

wiggled her fingers at the child and gave me a shrug. "Sorry! My bad!"

Rusty sat back on his haunches and laughed, Adriana cackling by his side.

What? He's a magical dog, I'm telling you!

Wait. Who's Guy?

CHAPTER 7

I wound up heading to Joe's Diner with Pandora and Adriana. We were going to meet my mom, Adelaide, and discuss the hellhounds and missing townsfolk. Lorcan was staying behind with Jake to help Sheriff Glen and a few other witches erase the tourists' memories and get things back in order. Pandora was ravenous, something that I had noticed was her usual condition, and I feared she'd begin eating her own arm if we didn't get something in her but quick.

When we walked into the diner, we found a harried Janelle running from booths to the register and back, checking out customers and serving others with her only help coming from a surly-looking teenager. Sheila was nowhere in sight, and I didn't expect her to be waitressing what with Gordy one of the missing.

Janelle was a new waitress and appeared almost as young as the teen who was stuffing straws into a receptacle. However, Sheila had informed us Janelle was in her mid-thirties. I didn't know if she was a witch—this would explain her youthful mien. I never did get around to finding out how to detect this magically, or how to ask politely if someone was a witch—and have a spell ready to remove the memory if the person in question was human. Even though I was progressing nicely and proficient for the most part in my spell casting, I still had years of missed arcane knowledge to catch up on.

"Adelaide is in the far corner booth," said Janelle as she rushed by with a platter, "I'll be with you ladies in a minute. Gabby! Take booth twelve a refill of coffee. Stop fiddling with those straws!" She turned to us and rolled her eyes then huffed out an exasperated, "Kids!"

We shot her smiles of sympathy then joined my mother who was waving at us from the back of the diner. As we passed the kitchen, I winked at Joe who was busy cooking up a storm. He barely nodded and I knew he'd not be taking the time to stop at our table for a chat. Summer tourism season made the residents and those in the service industry go into high gear. No time for social niceties with these crowds! I knew June Carter was pulling her hair out looking for summer help especially since Rowan Nightingale was locked away in the mental ward at the witch hospital—or was anyway if the report she's gone missing is to be believed.

"Addy! Did you have trouble keeping people from wanting to share the booth with you? Sorry we are late. I had to send someone to the pit of hell that was long overdue for a visit." Pandora didn't lower her voice and I quickly glanced around to see what the tourists thought of her comment. Since no one was looking askance her way, I assumed the glamour the Council put on our town was in full force, and the humans couldn't understand us when we spoke of anything paranormal.

Dorie was about to take the seat facing the front of the diner, but I scooted around her forcing her to take the seat facing the opposite way next to Adriana. She arched one eyebrow at me, but I scolded her once more. "The way you sit, you'll be giving everyone the full Sharon Stone since you are lacking in the underwear department."

"Oh, pooh. You are such a prude."

"Well, be that as it may, aren't you worried about the sanitary aspects of having your hoo-ha business touch every surface you place it on?" I asked.

Pandora gave me a wide grin and said, "Oh, so cute. Lily can't even use grown-up words to describe her..."

"Dorie!"

Adriana's shoulders were rocking in unbridled amusement.

I pointed my finger at her nose and chastised her attitude. "You stop. All you do is encourage her behavior and it just makes things worse."

I closed my eyes and began to rub my temples. When I opened them again, I jumped back in shock when I found my cat, Wicked, sitting on the table inches from my face.

"How did you...? No, I'm not even going to ask. Get off the table before someone complains," I grumbled.

Adelaide scooped Wicked up and placed her on the vinyl bench seat between us, where she promptly curled up and began to wash. I won't tell you where she was washing nor that she was facing it toward me.

"Who did you dispatch, Dorie?" Adelaide asked the crossroads demon.

"Old Greg is no longer with us. Part of me is going to miss that old coot," said Adriana.

"OK, ladies. What can I get you?" A frazzled Janelle came rushing back to our table and paused, pen to pad, waiting to hear our selections.

"Burger, fries, and sweet tea for me," I stated.

"I'll have the same, but I'd like the sweet potato fries," said Adelaide.

"Make mine a cheeseburger, but I want the chili fries—regular, not the sweet variety—and bring me a coffee," Adriana stated.

Pandora was looking over the menu like someone who'd been on a deserted island for the last four weeks with nothing to eat but coconuts.

"I'm not *too* hungry," she began, "so I think I will have a burger, rare, no cheese, mayo on the side. I want fries—no, onion rings. No, wait. Oh, just bring both. Then I want a cup of French onion soup—no, make it a bowl—extra French bread to sop up the broth. Do you have hot dogs? Oh, awesome! I want three. There they are! I didn't see them on the menu. I will take a NY coney style, a Chicago dog, and a Seattle dog—and put extra cream cheese on that one. Then I will have a slice of lemon meringue pie and some coffee. But first, bring me a glass of sweet tea. It's addictive!"

The surrounding tables got deathly still, and the people were now openly staring at Dorie as her words registered. By now, I was used to how much food she could pack away. But the general populace held her dining habits and the gusto with which she attacked her meals with shock and awe. Just sitting and perusing the menu, she's already managed to consume three buttered rolls and drunk all of our water.

By the time Janelle returned with our food piled high on a tray, she'd called Gabby over to help who was now struggling under the weight of her own tray that consisted of all of Pandora's choices. I couldn't help but notice every time the teen placed a dish in front of Dorie, the crossroads demon would lean in and sniff—Gabby, not the food. As the teen placed the last item on the table, Dorie reached out and grabbed Gabby's wrist and began to sniff from wrist to crook of the elbow. When she went to move higher up I cleared my throat to get Pandora's attention but failed.

"Um, Dorie? Do you think you could stop sniffing our waitress and concentrate on your food?"

"Huh? Oh! Sorry. I get them confused sometimes."

Gabby hurried away, following Janelle to the front of the diner where they began whispering furiously at the cash register. I couldn't help but notice they kept tracking their eyes in Pandora's direction.

Sigh.

We needed to talk. And soon.

Just as I took a large bite of my burger, Edith popped in and squeezed into the empty place between Adelaide and Adriana—not that anyone could see her but me and my great-grandmother.

"Hello, Edith," Adelaide said.

OK, so my mother could see ghosts as well.

"I adore your outfit, Edie, it's so salvage-yard chic," remarked Dorie with a snicker.

OK, so Pandora could obviously see ghosts as well. But she didn't need to taunt Edith. The poor ghost was forever stuck wearing the same outfit she'd had on when she met her end in Rowdy Harpin's salvage yard a few months back, hence Pandora's ribbing her about it.

Edith ignored Pandora and leaned forward, obviously about to dish some dirt she was privy to and eager to be the first one to tell us.

"I was about to head to your place when I got distracted by that nasty Greg and his shenanigans, may he rot in hell. Anyway, the reason I needed to speak to you

Lily, was about the news I found out this morning. Olivia is missing!"

"Ogden-Meyers? That Olivia?" Adriana asked in astonishment.

"Yes, *that* Olivia. Can you believe it? What is going on around here?" Edith cried.

"Pandora thinks the coven that has my dad have sent a scout or two our way and they are messing with us to let us know they mean business," I informed the ghost.

Edith barely glanced at Pandora then shrugged, "Perhaps. Or maybe Deanna is here already and camping out in the woods north of town. I saw some shimmery lights in that direction last night, but I couldn't investigate. Apparently I can't leave the town's perimeter otherwise I'd be more informed," she groused.

"That is something we can tackle tonight," said Adriana with a dark glance around the table. "If Deanna is here and has Charles, those renegade Romanos with her are more idiotic than I surmised."

"Most of these witches are related to you in some way, are they not?" asked Edith.

Adriana nodded and fussed with her napkin, frustration evident, especially as she had not wiped her plate clean yet. Only Adriana is second to Dorie in her ability to put away pounds of food in one sitting.

"They *are* part of the Romano clan in some way. And since they tend to intermarry, we are dealing with a coven of inbred cousins hellbent on eradicating the last of my family. Lucretia wasn't the only one set on this path. I just don't understand how I didn't know my lineage to such an extent that I missed how mixed in Breed we are. And not just the Romano and Dolce side—you Croys are a mishmash of Breed as well." Adriana addressed this last bit to Adelaide. "The question is, what does this mean? And how will it affect us remaining in power when all the dust settles and we manage to eradicate this threat and get Charles back," Adriana wondered.

"But why should it matter?" I asked. "What's the big deal? So, I have siren blood. And more." I glanced at Pandora unsure if I should mention our shared connection.

"It just isn't done, Lily," Adriana declared.

Adelaide looked down at her hands then over to me. "Lily, darling. The Breed never used to mix blood with other paranormals. Witches married witches. Sirens the same. Vampires with vampires and so on. A lot of this has to do with the fact we just don't know what mixed blood would produce. What kind of hybrid paranormal would be the result and would it negate some powers? Or *enhance* those powers incredibly, so that this new Breed, as a result, would be something to fear. Do you understand?"

No, I didn't understand. But I would accept that this was the way of the paranormal world and would worry about changing the minds of those who were offended by us mutts at a later date. I had my hands full right now.

"Lucretia is a prime example of someone who ran with the muddled blood and even enhanced herself by making a deal with this one here." Adriana jerked her thumb at Dorie who gave her a wink.

"I wish you could have seen the look on Lucretia's face when I nabbed her soul. It was one for the ages," Pandora replied.

"She is truly gone then?" Adelaide worried at her lower lip and looked to Pandora for confirmation.

"As much as I can tell. I mean, I recognized her soul and took it away, sending it where it belongs. But something black and inky slithered away and Valgaard did say he wrested the vampirism part leaving her vulnerable to attack. You saw what that did, Addy, it was you who threw the knife that ended her." Pandora stretched and the buttons on her shirt threatened to pop off with the strain. A man at the next table began choking on his meal and his wife, who'd been observing him eying Dorie's curves with mild irritation, smacked him hard on the back of his head with her purse. Not quite the Heimlich maneuver, but it worked. He spit up whatever he'd been choking on and took a drink of water, avoiding our eyes in the process.

Pandora wiggled her fingers at the woman and bared her teeth.

The wife hurriedly turned away and focused on her plate while quietly scolding her spouse.

Dorie chuckled. Such a menace.

"I hope Lucretia doesn't come back as some great undead threat then. I don't like that a part of her slipped into the ether. Even if she is ripped into shreds and weak. Why can't things be as simple as Harry killing Voldmort?" I complained.

All three women at the table gave me equal stares of confusion, but Edith chuckled in understanding. My mother had been trapped inside of a cat for the last twenty years, Pandora in her book prison, and Adriana? Well, she had no excuse other than the fact she chose to spend her time creating her own dark arts and didn't have the time to watch movies or read the books they were based on, I guessed.

"Never mind," I said, then turned to Dorie. "Is that the main reason Lucretia wanted you all those years back when my mom, dad, and Aunt Jessica were kids? To destroy you in book form and remove the threat of you taking her soul?"

Pandora nodded, her platinum-streaked golden locks cascading around her shoulders, having been released from her ponytail when she'd rounded up Old Greg. "That and my blood ties to all of you. She wanted total elimination of any vestige of Dolce, Croy, Romano, and Fortune blood. And that meant *you* were her prime target. Once she had her hands on me, I could be Charlie's downfall."

Adelaide's fork clanged loudly on her plate, and she stared at Pandora in shock, waiting for the crossroads demon to further elaborate.

"So... that's sort of what I discovered on my little jaunt across the country—and boy was it difficult keeping Deanna from sensing my presence! I had to tread carefully to glean that information from Charlie and another coven member. The reason Charlie is still alive is twofold. One, Deanna wants him as her paramour and she kept him from Lucretia who she'd betrayed along with Donna. Deanna has been double agenting everyone who had a hand in this mess." Pandora pushed her last plate away and took a sip of tea before continuing.

"Lucretia had been trying to find out where Charlie was taken. She was independent of the Romano coven out west—utterly and emphatically an outcast and renegade witch. The Italian side of the family would have hunted her down and tried to destroy her had they known she was still alive and among us, causing trouble for all these years, even though they have blood on their *own* hands, so to speak." Pandora leaned forward as she continued with her tale.

"When Deanna spelled Charlie, she put a blood curse on him that is so dark and vile, even I shudder at what it's done to him."

Adriana had such a firm grip on her utensils I thought they might bend in her anger. Instead, she slammed her hands down on the table then balled them into fists. "Did Deanna put the Black Oath Curse on Charlie?" she asked.

"Worse." Pandora looked so woebegone, I began to tremble in the wake of her agitated and worried demeanor.

I wasn't sure what all these spells meant, but the level of hubris my great-grandmother placed on her query made me realize the Black Oath Curse must be truly awful. But if Dorie insisted this other magic was even worse? I shuddered at the thought of what it meant for my dad—and us.

"What could be worse?" asked Adelaide.

"Deanna hit Charlie with the Sangua Percutiens Primogenita Mori."

Edith crossed herself and Adelaide and Adriana looked as if they'd faint dead away. Adriana closed her eyes and shook her head. My mother placed a hand over her heart and looked so distressed I reached out to comfort her. Even Wicked growled and flattened herself on the seat.

"I'm sorry. What kind of spell is that? What does it mean?" I asked.

"It's not a spell," Pandora explained, "It's a curse. It loosely translates to Blood of Firstborn Death Strike. You, through me, were the means to destroy Charlie, Lily. Because we share blood—demon blood. The curse would have traveled through me in book form and not only eliminated Charlie but every living and breathing one of your relatives far and wide. Everyone would have been wiped out in an instant."

"But that's...it's OK, then. I mean...Lucretia is dead, and you aren't a book. What's the problem here?" I asked in a puzzled voice.

"It means freeing Pandora has released the first part of the curse. Lucretia wanted to destroy my direct line...but Deanna? She wants to wipe the planet of us all. Lucretia would have stopped that threat by destroying Dorie then worked her way to Charlie, Adelaide, Antonio, me and then you, Lily. Now that Pandora is loose, it triggered the curse. Only we have no idea what the next part is. None at all."

Well, isn't *that* special. Not.

CHAPTER 8

I was lying across the sofa in my den. I tried to relax and remain calm, but this wasn't easily accomplished with Andrea chattering nervously, her mind overloaded with everything we'd been discussing and her lobbing question-after-question my way.

Lorcan was rubbing my feet, and while I was still miffed with him—yeah, foot rub.

Pandora was randomly opening and closing my cabinets looking for something to eat. I needed to do something about her voracious appetite otherwise I'd go broke trying to keep up with her gluttony. I'd mentioned the possibility of getting more pastries from Steve Junior but she shied away from that idea which had me highly suspicious. Dorie seemed to love Steve—*and* his pastries—so I wondered what had happened to cause her sudden change in attitude. Whatever it was, it couldn't be a good thing.

"Can you stop snacking so loudly, Dorie? What are you munching on anyway?"

"I don't know, these tiny crunchy things. They taste like feet."

I rose up and stared at the bag in Pandora's hand.

"That's cat food."

Dorie shrugged and continued munching. Wicked was at her feet snatching up the bits Pandora dropped by accident.

"When is Adriana arriving with the hellhounds?" Lorcan asked.

This entire hellhound idea had me worried beyond reason. I mean, hell and hound usually meant huge vicious beasts that would slaughter anything and everything in their wake, right? So why everyone was so calm about these nasty pooches was beyond the scope of my understanding. Adelaide has taken to her bed, declaring she'd found herself with a mild headache after lunch. But I knew she was trying to deal with the realization that we had a heap of trouble on our hands with this curse issue. I didn't blame her for tossing the covers over her head and pretending the world didn't exist.

I wanted to join her.

Instead, I slipped my feet from Lorcan's ministrations and wandered to my back door peering out at my yard. Turning the knob, I walked onto my side porch glancing around. Wicked followed me outside and scampered off around the side of my house despite the gentle rain coming down. My vegetable garden was flourishing. Abner had done well, his nurturing care evident everywhere I looked. Vegetables were just hinting at how abundant they'd become as I spied a few in and among the leafy plants to which they were attached. Flowers were in full bloom, including the sweetbriar rose bush and the falling rain which picked up in intensity now, began to accumulate on the stepping-stones, their droplets also landing in crevices and valleys on leaves and petals.

My yard, obviously transformed from the sad state it

had been just a few months ago, was now something of which to be proud.

I heard the baying hounds before I saw Old Frank's pickup truck, Adriana riding shotgun with the windows down, as it pulled into my drive. I couldn't exactly see the dogs because they were in the largest crates ever know in the canine world—and they were covered in burlap. I guess this was to protect the tourists from catching a glimpse inside.

I mean, how many times can you wipe a human's memory before they got all wonky and wound up spouting odd tales to the National Enquirer. *Hmmm...I wonder.*

I observed Old Frank getting out of his truck and uncovering the layers that hid the beasts from sight, and it occurred to me he might be mourning Old Greg. Even with the acrimony between the two, Greg *was* his older brother after all and now resided in hell. But one could never tell with Frank. I wondered why everyone used 'old' before stating their names but why Abner didn't garner the same moniker. Perhaps it was better I didn't know that answer. Especially since I couldn't imagine calling him *Young* Abner.

"Bring them inside, Frank. The weather out here is miserable." Adriana came striding over to me looking self-satisfied, like what I was about to experience would be nothing short of magnificent and it was all due to her scheming. "Wait until you meet the boys. They have grown some since the last time I saw them."

Lovely. Wait. *Inside?* Like, my *house?*

Eileen and Henry Reid came through our shared gate just then, both holding baskets of berries freshly picked from their garden. Eileen had raspberries and Henry had the same only his were a unique golden variety he promised were even more delicious than their red counterpart. They came and stood by Adriana and me and collectively we watched as Old Frank let the hounds out of their cages and into my yard. Lorcan, Andrea, and Pandora came outside to watch the show as well—Dorie still munching on cat food.

"Holy heck. What in heaven's name are those two things?" I remained transfixed, my mouth hanging open and my eyes bugging out. One conjures images in their mind when they hear *hellhounds,* and I would think big, black, brutes and sharp white teeth would be front and center as descriptors. But these monsters were nothing like anything I'd ever laid eyes on in my short time on this planet.

"Are they? But I don't...wait a minute. They're purple? The hellhounds are *purple?*" I was gobsmacked.

"More like a dark puce, but yeah," chuckled Pandora.

"I think they look like the darkest shade of mauve in existence," added Andrea, trying to be helpful.

"I had a car in the '80s that color," Henry reminisced and rubbed his chin. "Well, maybe these lads are a tad darker."

Lads? *Lads?* These were demon spawn troglodytes with yellow teeth and eyes the color of dripping blood. When they scented the air, it sounded like those dinosaurs in Jurassic Park that still give me nightmares every time I recall them. These creatures were hardly lads!

"Max! Come. No, Rex. Stop that."

Too late for Old Frank's commands to reach their assuredly pea-sized brains, Max and Rex proceeded to lift their legs on the tires of my Jeep and let out a stream so foul-scented and unending, we all looked on in amazement at the water show.

Their ablutions complete, both hounds noticed their audience and began to growl at us. Again, nothing on this planet came close to comparing the noise I was hearing, although it did remind me of the Balrog in the Lord of the Rings trilogy. These two were almost as big. Max, or what I thought might be the hound with that name, easily stood as tall as my Jeep, and Rex—his brother, I assume—was an inch or two shorter. It was akin to having two rhinoceros in my garden only instead of horns, they had razer-sharp stiletto daggers coming out of their mouths.

Just as Frank managed to bring them toward us for introductions—or the massacre I was certain would occur once they reach our side—the unexpected happened. Or really, I say *unexpected,* but did one really not see this coming a mile away and wonder that no one had thought to do something as a preventative earlier so we could have avoided it?

And what had me sucking my breath in so quickly and deeply the oxygen levels in my yard plummeted by a few percentage points?

Wicked chose that moment to return.

The consequent encounter made that scene in Kill Bill where Beatrix battles the Crazy 88 seem like school kids playing Capture the Flag. In other words—it was a gorefest.

"I've never seen so much blood in one area at one time." I was rocking back and forth in my den with Lorcan by my side trying to soothe my traumatized nerves. The horror at what I just witnessed wouldn't let me settle long enough for him to work his empath magic on me.

Andrea was still crying.

Eileen was handing out tea—the red splotches all over

her shirt bearing witness to the fracas that ensued. Henry was yellow.

No, I don't mean he was a coward. His shirt. It was yellow from where his prized golden raspberries smushed into it as the massive dogs slammed into him trying to escape the claws of death.

I could still hear the howling in my mind. From the hellhounds—not Henry. I don't think I will ever forget the sounds of distress coming out of the duo.

The noise Wicked made was the stuff of nightmares. The wails and caterwauls from the deepest, darkest levels of Hades couldn't compare to the noise she made when both Max and Rex lunged at her. They got within an inch of her face, jaws snapping and saliva flying in all directions, when my tiny black furball morphed into that Zuni warrior doll from Trilogy of Terror. I kid you not.

If two denizens of the underworld could stop on a dime, turn, and take flight any faster than those two giant mongrels did, I would eat my hat. They couldn't escape anywhere seeing as how they were tethered to a cowering Frank, so all they managed to do was loop around the poor man three times before they slammed heads and went down in a colossal heap. Frank was under them.

This was a good thing because Wicked began her assault in earnest, ricocheting back and forth in a demented boomerang ninja kind of way, going from haunch to withers to neck to head and back down the length of the two dogs. Until the gashes from her claws made a fountain of blood so prolific it would make Old Faithful jealous.

We had to call Doc Holcomb to my place for an emergency visit. Max and Rex had forty stitches each and were on medication to keep them calm—so wrecked were they from their ordeal. Wicked was nonchalantly washing herself up on her favorite perch in my sunroom and had nary a scratch or bruise—if you discounted the copious amount of sticky green blood from the hellhounds covering her fur.

Yes, they bled green.

No, I was not about to wash the cat. Would you?

I sat up and a raspberry fell from my hair. I let it be. Henry was wiping his shirt and making tsking sounds at the berry loss—or maybe he was just tsking in general at the recent pandemonium he'd lived through. I was thrilled he hadn't lost his dentures this time around. Just the thought of him picking them up and wiping off the green globs of blood before shoving them back in his mouth made me gag a little.

"Lordy. And I thought I'd seen it all when you brought that young lady into my vet office last year. Seems she has gotten meaner since the last time we met." Doc Holcomb observed the fierce little furball who sneezed then squinted his way.

"Just send me the bill," was all I could manage to squeak out.

"Doc Holcomb, any word on Keisha?" Andrea had recovered enough to remember her manners, although she had snot boogers on her nose and was using a tissue that had seen better days to try and mop them up. I wanted to kick myself for forgetting to ask the man about his daughter.

"Nothing. The sheriff and his team are going above and beyond, but we don't know what has happened to her and any of the others. I've not slept a wink since I heard the news."

Lorcan reached out and clasped the man's shoulder, and I knew he sent some empath energy coursing into the vet. It would help some, but nothing would make Doc

Holcomb return to his usually mild-mannered, agreeable self until the return of Keisha.

"Don't worry, Doc. Once we get the boys back in line, and the medication wears off a bit, we intend to have them sniff out whoever has taken those missing from our town, Keisha included," said Adriana. "I will certainly make sure whoever did this will regret ever coming to our town," she added darkly.

After the vet left, we gave the hounds fresh water and about fifteen steaks apiece and left them to sleep it off on my side porch. They were safely locked in their crates to prevent further harm lest Wicked decided to torture them again.

"Do you think you will ever get their blood off your porch?" Andrea asked.

"Probably not. I can always paint the house trim green to match. What I would like to know is, if those two are our best hope in tracking the bad guys, what do we do with them if the enemy has their own fiendish felines to go on the attack? Max and Rex are probably ruined—their reputations will be once word gets out about this little episode—and it *will* get out," I remarked.

"We've got more problems than worrying about those two dogs," said Pandora ominously. She'd just charged into the kitchen after disappearing upstairs and I jumped when she made that announcement since I was focused on Wicked and didn't hear her approach.

"Why? What's wrong now?" I asked.

"It's Adelaide. Didn't any of you wonder when she didn't come downstairs in all the hullabaloo?" Pandora explained.

Oh my gosh! Was she gone? Did the bad guys sneak into my home and kidnap her as well?

"Please tell me she isn't missing!" I cried.

Pandora shook her head no, but had such a somber look on her face, I knew I wouldn't like what she was about to say.

"No. She's upstairs in bed," Dorie replied. "However, she is in some kind of trance, and I can't wake her. There are two things that have me worried. One, it looks like she's back in her coma-like state, and this time she's not lying all peaceful. I can tell she is struggling but unable to awaken. This is *not* a good thing."

"I understand, I mean, I can see why this is bad news. By what's the second thing that has you worried? You haven't said yet," asked Andrea.

"Second," said Pandora, holding up two fingers, "I believe she is in a battle of wills with Deanna Fredricks, because I heard her yell out Charlie's name, and then she said, 'You bitch!' "

Oh, well, this is accelerating things at an already alarming rate. What were we sitting around here waiting for? It was time for action!

I just didn't know what the heck we were going to do about this turn of events yet.

"Lorcan, go fetch your truck," ordered Adriana, "I have a witch I need to speak with."

My great-grandmother flashed a glare around the room that would freeze flowing water, so glacial was her demeanor. I didn't envy whoever she was about to confront.

Not one bit.

CHAPTER 9

"We have a missing Rowan Nightingale, which I suspect was a breakout not a kidnapping," stated Adriana. "Despite what Samantha is insisting, we know they are both in this up to their eyeballs and Rowan is no innocent. She is a diabolical lunatic."

I nodded in agreement.

Adriana and Lorcan had returned from their visit to the prison, now easily accessible to my family after I made a few heads roll despite my lowly stature as a non-Elder. Being a dark witch had its perks, one of them being fear-mongering. I didn't care who I frightened as long as I got what I wanted. My, how quickly I've changed.

"Is there any rhyme or reason to the choices in victims? I mean, we have Gordy Polk, Olivia Ogden-Meyers, Mary Lee and Nathan Jacobs, Martha Mosely, and Keisha Holcomb. They are all friends and acquaintances, but I don't see any pattern, really." I offered.

"I don't think there is a pattern. Just random people we know being kidnapped because we know them." Adriana looked flustered and I knew she was worried about our friends—so was I. "We stopped in at the mental ward of the hospital and questioned the guards, I'll have you know. No one saw anything and the closed-circuit cameras were hit with magic because they go black during the time before and during Rowan's escape. They don't come back on for an hour."

Samantha Fairburn was Rowan's aunt, and both of them were guilty of aiding and abetting Donna and Deanna. Although it seems Donna had been hoodwinked by her sibling, and Samantha helped Deanna with the deception and deceit. Rowan was no better.

The doorbell rang, startling us and I hoped it wasn't Tiffany Clarkson of the Sweet Briar Clarksons returning to say the neighbors complained once more over the recent disturbance—although in all honesty, I wouldn't blame them if they did. How could I? It sounded like World War III had just occurred and anyone in their right mind would call the authorities to check it out.

However, when I opened the door, I found Shirley Jones standing there wringing her hands and looking like she'd just had a good, long cryfest.

"Shirley! Why are you at my front door? Friends come in the back! You know that!" I scolded gently. The poor dear looked like anything harsher, and she'd fall apart in a blubbering mess. "Shirley! What is it?" I asked, troubled when her face crumbled at my query.

"Oh, Lily. I did something bad. I needed to come tell y'all and get it off my chest. But...well, I'm afraid y'all are going to hate me when you hear what I have to say!" I led our town's trusted EMT to the kitchen and settled her in a chair while Andrea put a cup of hot tea down in front of her. Shirley's bouffant dishwater-blonde hair was askew, and her '70s makeup swank looked more like she'd ridden with her head hanging out the window through a car wash so smudged was her face.

"Drink up, dear. You will feel better," said Eileen.

Just then, the cleric Adriana and Lorcan had obtained at the hospital to examine Adelaide, came downstairs and into the kitchen.

"I've never seen anything like this," she declared. "Adelaide is non-responsive to anything I do to her, yet it is obvious to anyone looking at her she is fighting someone. She strains and pulls, then sighs and goes quiet, only to start up again in a few minutes. I don't know if it's all in her head or if she's really at risk!"

My Aunt Iona was upstairs after we called to inform her that we discovered my mom had gone under a spell again. I knew she wouldn't leave my mother's side and it freed me to concentrate on what we needed to do next to fight this threat and bring the battle to Deanna.

I felt the urgency and knew we were running out of time.

Adriana walked over to the cleric and shook her hand. "It's OK, Nellie. You can only do so much. We don't have all the answers yet and you've made Addy as comfortable as possible. We will figure this out."

With that, Nellie the cleric wished us a good night and left.

Turning our attention back to Shirley, we waited for her to begin her tale.

"A few weeks back, I was approached by a man. He was sort of ordinary. What I mean is, if I had to describe him to you now, I'd have a difficult time of it. Medium to light brown hair, rather pale, average height, average weight, medium brown eyes, and nothing on him even remotely remarkable that stands out."

Andrea was taking notes but paused, lightly tapping

her pen on the table, waiting breathlessly like a reporter in an interview. Edith was taking notes as well, only I could see through her pad and pencil.

"He introduced himself, said his name was Alan, and asked me if I'd like to show him around town since he was new to our area, here for the spring festival. This was two weeks back...the weekend before Memorial Day. Our tourism was picking up what with the new fairgrounds and all, he said he liked to do arts and crafts and maybe he would consider renting a booth," said Shirley.

I was momentarily distracted when my thoughts ran to the booth rentals and my setup. I had my younger cousin Fiona, she of the graduation and college future, and one of her friends working my *Found Things* booth since I never seemed to have the time to do it myself. I'd been lucky in that Fiona wanted to raise as much money as she could before the end of August when she'd be off to Brenau University down in Gainesville, and happily did a bang-up job for me. I longed for the days when I could create some spectacular folk art pieces and spend my weekends hawking my wares in my artsy booth instead of chasing evil around every corner. But right now, I needed to focus on what Shirley was telling us.

"...So we went for coffee. The next thing I knew, I became confused and couldn't sleep at night. I had anxiety attacks and my tummy remained in a constant state of turmoil," Shirley finished.

Adriana looked at Shirley with little patience and plenty of exasperation. "But why is any of this our concern? I don't mean to sound callous, woman, but we have people missing and now Adelaide in some kind of sleeping spell again. Why did you come here with this information—what little there is?"

"That's just it! Over the last few days, I began to

remember things I must have forgotten—or if what I'm thinking occurred—was made to forget." Shirley sat forward placing both hands on my kitchen table and her voice rose a hitch. "That man began asking me about the townsfolk and somehow your name came up, Lily. When he casually asked me about who did what around here, I mentioned some people and what their occupations were and such. He seemed mildly interested but not in a way which made me suspicious. Alan even gave me his business card which I've brought with me. Now that my memory is less fuzzy, I realized the very people I mentioned to the man are the same ones who are now missing! I think he might be behind the abductions!" she cried.

Now we were getting somewhere!

We thanked Shirley, sending her on her way, with a few extra hugs and promises she did a good thing by unburdening herself to us. We also inferred she was in no way responsible for any of this and encouraged her to not blame herself. Before she departed, Edith had a great idea, suggesting that Shirley stop in at the hospital where she worked and have the druids do a magical brain scan to see if her memories could be retrieved—with the possibility she might be able to ID this man should they cross paths again.

We were back in my den minus Eileen and Henry, who left with Shirley and were now at home assuredly changing their clothes. I'm sure they were lamenting the loss of their raspberries as well. After a quick check by me to assure Adelaide was as fine as someone in a Sleeping Beauty state could be, I settled back on the sofa, feet once more tucked in Lorcan's capable hands and scrutinized the business card.

"Gotta sniff it."

I jumped when I realized the voice belonged to Old Frank. *Was he still here?*

"Who? Dorie?" I mean, she sniffed that young waitress, so my mind immediately went there.

"Uh...no, ma'am. Them dogs. Let them sniff the card," he said.

The dogs!

We all stood and ran to my side porch where the hell-hounds were safely tucked away from the wicked claws of Wicked. She didn't seem at all agitated now, and I suspect she went off on a tangent just to throw some excitement into my day.

She's ornery like that.

Pandora reached Max and Rex first and let them out. Unlike Old Frank's regular pooches, these two couldn't get enough of Dorie. They wriggled, whined, and rolled over for belly rubs which was saying something considering they were the size of small tanks.

"Who's my good boy? Is it you Rexy? Or you, Max? Huh? Who's the good doggy?" Pandora was using her long nails like a comb and Max—or was it Rex? —was thumping his leg in ecstasy at her belly-rubbing technique. They were slightly groggy but steady on their feet.

I noticed Abner tending my garden and he sniffed when he noticed his brother, and turning away, began to work the soil. I'd have to inform him later about Greg, since I doubted Frank would, but for now, I wondered at his attitude. I wanted to get to the bottom of why these two didn't get along. It couldn't be because Frank made moon-shine illegally somewhere up in the hills. There had to be another reason for it. I thought Adriana mentioned some-thing about a still explosion and a pet pig, but I could never trust anything that came out of that woman's mouth.

"Dorie, can you please quit it? Let me have the dogs

get a whiff of this business card and see where it goes," I said.

We spent a good fifteen minutes staring at the small white rectangle with the name Alan Webb printed across the front. Just under it was a phone number. Adriana used her cell phone to call it, which I'd discouraged, but it went through to a customer service line for Amazon. As much as I thought Alan was downplaying his true intent for being here, I couldn't see the man splitting his time between the shipping/shopping giant and world domination—or in our case, kidnapping Sweet Briar residents. We concluded it was a ruse.

Tentatively reaching my hand out with the card dangling from one end, I waved it in front of the nose of the first hound, then did the same with the other. They regarded me curiously then began to sniff the slip of paper making snuffling noises and drooling long strings of saliva which reached the ground forming puddles.

Then both dogs growled. Followed by baying that came straight out of a Stephen King novel, although I was certain Cujo had nothing on these two.

CHAPTER 10

"I didn't believe we'd find anything out here, but those *are* shimmering lights. Edith was right," I said.

"I still don't know why we had to sneak out and leave the men behind," whined Andrea. She'd been saying things like that for the last ten minutes and it was getting on my nerves. I loved my cousin, but she tended to worry incessantly and was scratching her elbows raw.

"We don't need the men to protect us. They will just get in the way." Adriana sniffed and rubbed her chin while considering our next move.

Speaking of protection, the town had gone on lock-down mode, and everyone who was in the position to guard those of a lesser caliber in witchcraft was doing their duty by keeping an eye on their friends and neighbors. Adriana finally brought Mortimer in the loop, but he informed her he was up in North Carolina with our Fortune cousins of all things and sent a few werewolf friends over to my great-grandparents' house to protect Antonio. He was teaching the extra shaggy dudes how to play Scopa—his favorite Italian card game—and telling them off-colored jokes, I'm sure.

In other words, Antonio was safe so Adriana could concentrate on fighting evil. She was ready for battle.

No, really.

In lieu of her standard winter detective garb that did little to make her look even remotely like Sherlock Holmes or Hercule Poirot or even Miss Marple, Adriana was now in what she deemed 'summer ninja wear,' and our eyes were forever ruined with the imagery imbedded in them.

"Did you realize those capri pants are see-through?" I asked, trying not to look at the wreckage that would surely put me off my diet for weeks.

"They are not."

"Are too."

"Are not, dummy."

"Are too. You are delusional."

"Not. You are imagining things."

"Are too. I can *see* everything."

"And you are looking why?"

Adriana had me there.

"Would you two stop it? It's not like anyone is going to see her in that getup. Not unless we stumble upon an encampment of rogue witches, and they are the type to give fashion tips." Pandora decided to tag along, much to the disappointment of Edith who I'm sure felt left out. Dorie's ensemble was even more outlandish.

"She is wearing a red thong," I mouthed to both Dorie and Andrea who couldn't help but stare at my great-grand-mother's behind.

"Your capri pants *are* see-through," chided Pandora.

"Stuff it."

"See? Delusional—and grumpy." Turning to Pandora, I happened to glance down at her foot attire.

"Can I ask how you manage to walk through dirt and loam in stilettos and not sink into the ground?"

"I walk on my toes," Dorie replied.

"And they don't ache?" I asked.

"Not really."

"Not even a bit?"

"You should try walking through hell barefoot."

Um, no thanks, though she had a point.

The rest of Pandora's outfit consisted of tight black shorts, a tight button-up shirt where she'd undone the lower buttons and tied it in a knot exposing her midriff, with her hair up in a high ponytail. Andrea and I looked boring in our jeans and matching black tees.

Adriana began walking once more and we tagged along behind her. Andrea dropped back and whispered furiously. "Do you see her top? I think it a bustier from the '80s. She's still wearing those hiking boots she picked up at Goodwill, and they are two sizes too large! And what's with that headband?" she asked.

"It's a Japanese hachimaki headband with the rising run on it," Pandora snickered. "She looks like a cross-dressing Karate Kid!"

"I heard that."

We all goggled at each other and stifled our giggles.

"I don't think I can get past the fact that Granny has some major boobage still...and at her age!" I whispered.

"I heard that, too!"

I folded my lips in and made a zipping motion and the other two women nodded. No way did we want to get on Adriana's bad side, especially in her current mood which was dialed toward diabolical.

"What's the plan when we reach the lights?" I asked in a hushed voice lest it carried and alerted whoever was up ahead. Although now that I thought on it, I wondered if there would be scouts on the lookout for trespassers. Perhaps we should have cloaked ourselves with Andrea's magical abilities. I was just about to say something more when Adriana held her hand out motioning we should stop. So we did.

We stood still and waited. A light, welcoming breeze swirled through the trees making the leaves rustle, giving us some relief from the humidity which sprang up out of nowhere and carried the scent of something unidentifiable with it. I thought I detected the apples, but it was too early in the growing season for the fruit. The wind shifted and now I smelled bananas. What on earth?

"Stay away from any trees that look bent," whispered Adriana as she crept forward once more.

"Why?" I barely breathed the question out, and no one responded. I don't think anyone heard me to tell the truth.

"I hear bubbling up ahead. Like cauldrons or something. I think we found them!" Andrea was excited but nervous and I worried her elbows would be raw and bleeding if something didn't give soon.

"No. It's not...hmm," said Adriana quietly to herself.

We crouched and began the slow, arduous process of making our way through the pine trees and pin oaks trying to avoid the poison ivy which had suddenly and menacingly popped up out of nowhere. It was all around us and I began watching where I was stepping rather than looking ahead.

We went on like this for about another ten minutes when I smothered a yelp and began rubbing my ankle. Then my fingers and hands began throbbing equally in pain and I began to gasp. I noticed everyone but Dorie was doing the same and was worried we had stepped on a hornet's nest. Something was obviously biting us, but I couldn't see or hear what it could be!

"Ow! What is that? My legs are on fire! Is it fire ants?" The plague of the South, those tiny ants packed quite the punch, but dare I say this was even worse?

Pandora, who didn't seem affected at all by this mystery pain, leaned down to the ground and began to investigate. Straightening up, she gathered us close and whispered, "Stinging nettle. It's everywhere."

Holy cow! That plant would make anyone wish they were covered in yellow jackets! The pain was so intense! It usually lasted about fifteen minutes and your skin would blister and swell where it came in contact. Sleeping on a bed of poison ivy would be a relief.

"What do we do?" Andrea's voice hitched a bit louder, and I became alarmed. I did not want us to give away our position and find ourselves surrounded by the enemy, so I looked to Dorie for aid. Both she and Adriana rolled their eyes and waved their hands in front of themselves. Instantly the pain abated. Oh, yeah...use magic. Duh!

Placing her hands before her, Adriana let out a soft chant and the stinging nettle shriveled before our eyes replaced by the tiny blue flowers of forget-me-nots. That was a handy spell. I'd have to learn it at a later date.

We had just crept forward a few more feet when Adriana held up her hand once more. "Don't go any further. We have ourselves a..."

"Hey! That looks like Wicked! Oh my gosh! Did they capture her? I have to save my cat!"

Rushing forward without giving any thought to what I was doing, and despite Adriana reaching out to stop my forward momentum, I plowed through the underbrush and reached a small clearing just as I heard a snap and felt myself flung far into the air.

Letting out a shriek, I heard someone scream beside

me followed by the howl of wolves and a gunshot. Then everything went still.

Well, I say still, but I was slowly rocking back and forth in a massive net and could just make out Andrea in her own prison of a similar design. Below us stood Pandora and Adriana, the latter scowling, but Dorie had her head thrown back and she was laughing like a loon. That's when I saw the still in the moonlight and from various magic balls hovering in the glen. Standing next to the still was a wide-eyed Old Frank with Rusty by his side holding a shotgun. The rest of the pack was circling around the area and looked agitated.

Looking directly below me, my black eyes met the incredulous cerulean blue ones of one Brian Chase, detective, and too gorgeous for his own good.

What was he doing here?

❧

"SERIOUSLY, what are you doing out here? And why would Frank have a moonshine still just over the border in North Carolina? Doesn't he know it's illegal in both states?" I grumped and kept pulling twigs and brambles out of my hair. It was a losing battle—my dark locks had at least twenty burrs tangling them up in a hot mess.

"I'm out here for the same reason you four decided to make this little jaunt," said Brian. "The light. Only I knew I was running Frank off and not launching an attack on an enemy coven the size of which has yet to be determined. What were you thinking? No, wait...you weren't thinking!"

"Oh, stop acting all superior. A renegade witch coven could have been out here. Just because it's Frank making 'shine doesn't mean we are imbeciles!" Adriana barked.

"And that makes it OK? Four of you against a

dangerous enemy?"

"We are the ones who are dangerous, mister. Well, with the exception of my great-granddaughter, Andrea. We brought her along to go with our cheese," Adriana stated dryly.

"Your cheese? I don't get—hey! I wasn't whining that much!" protested Andrea.

"Yet you were," Adriana sniffed.

"I just...oh, alright!" Andrea walked over to a larger boulder and sat down in a huff. "And I might not have any dark magic in me, but if we did run into a dangerous situation, who would have been able to cloak us all making us instantly invisible, huh?"

Wicked walked over and sat at my feet blinking up at me with a bored look on her face.

"And just what are you doing all the way up here, young lady? We are five miles from town. You're a cat. You should be at home curled up on my bed dreaming of terrorizing hellhounds not hanging around Old Frank's dog pack watching him make moonshine!"

"She's taken a shining to Rusty there." Frank nodded at his big, shaggy dog who was grinning, tongue hanging out and his tail doing a slow wag. "Every few nights when I drive through town, your cat comes running out of the bushes and waits for us to pick her up and take her with us."

How lovely.

"And you! Carrying a shotgun and shooting at us! How could you, Frank?" I scolded, crossing my arms over my chest.

"I didn't shoot at you! Wicked startled when you came barreling in the clearing and set off my traps. She jumped on me, my rifle accidentally went off and it didn't harm no one. Bullet went in that tree over there."

"You could have hurt my cat!" I wailed.

"Forget the cat. We have wasted enough time on this fool's errand. I knew I shouldn't have listened to Edith!" Adriana complained. "If you had just listened to me before taking off like a rabid squirrel, I was trying to explain how we'd made a mistake and found Frank's still. But no. You had to go after that cat. Serves you right winding up dangling like a dodo bird in that net!" Ariana was in a foul mood, and I really couldn't blame her.

We'd walked a mile and a half, in the woods, had poison ivy and stinging nettle attack us, and I was humiliated having gotten caught in Frank's booby trap. The man was a menace! I'm just glad Brian can shut down this little operation so it would be one less illegal moonshine operation for him to worry about.

"We still have Max and Rex, and they caught the scent of something on that business card. Tomorrow, well...it's already tomorrow...so later on today, we have plans to let them wander around town and see if they can pick up on a trail that Alan character may have left behind. This was a long shot at best," I stated, hoping it would improve Adriana's mood.

It didn't.

"We have to find the missing townsfolk. We have to find out who is behind this—well, we know who that is, but we need to stop running blind and have the upper hand for once. I'm sick of being in the dark and stumbling into clues or finding out truths either by accident or because some kind of monumental event occurs. We've been jerked around as a family for way too long. It's time to turn the tables." Adriana stood up and brushed off her pants then glared at Brian.

"We are parked a few miles back on Old Coleman River Road. How did you get here?" Adriana asked.

"I have my Grand Cherokee parked about twenty feet away from Lily's vehicle. That's how I knew you were out here."

"So that means another two-mile trek back. I was hoping there was a service road or something you'd driven up on so we could hitch a ride," I sighed.

Brian's eyes twinkled even as he hit Frank with a weighted look. Turning back to me, he dangled his keys in my face and smiled. "Oh, I just might have parked and took a look in your Jeep in the hopes I'd find you all listening to tunes or some other inane thing. When I didn't, I knew you'd be heading to this clearing to find out what the lights were about. So I drove up the old hunting trail. My vehicle is about one hundred feet in that direction." He nodded to our east and I almost whimpered so glad was I to not have to trudge all the way back through that mess of branches and weeds.

I scooped up Wicked and had to stop myself from doing a little happy dance and motioned to the others that it was time to head out.

"And as much as I'd love to take you ladies back to your car," Brian's voice stopped me in my tracks, "I need to dismantle Frank's moonshine operation and stick the parts in my vehicle—it's evidence you know."

My face fell and my shoulders drooped. I almost threw my cat at Brian's head. Turning on a dime, I began to make my way back down the path we'd carved into the woods, this time circumventing the area where I was certain more traps lie in wait. I could hear Brian chuckle as I strode past, and my mood darkened considerably.

I'd show him, getting my hopes up like that.

Didn't Brian realize I'd embraced my dark side? He better mind his manners!

CHAPTER 11

After a long hot shower and tossing my filthy clothing in the wash, I crawled into bed to try and get some sleep—but not before stopping in to check on my mom. Adelaide looked restful except for the slight wrinkle between her brows, a telltale sign that something was not quite right. I hoped she was in a dream state and nothing malevolent had occurred to bring her to where Deanna was camped with my dad.

What a nightmare—literally.

I draped a throw blanket over Aunt Iona who was lightly snoring in her recliner beside the bed. Despite the humidity outside, my AC was chugging along, and I felt a slight chill, so I assumed my aunt might awaken if she became cold. That task accomplished, I went back to my room.

I had a difficult time dropping off, but when sleep finally took over, I had disjointed dreams that had me tossing and turning. The imagery was unsettling, and my brain was working overtime to decipher all it was experiencing. I knew I was dreaming about Deanna and my dad, the coven, Adelaide—even Wicked showed up at one point and began walking on two legs, using her front paws to motion I should follow.

After a hectic and frenetic chase through deep woods and a brief interlude spent trying to cross a bubbling lake in a rickety boat where I'd discovered halfway across I was actually rowing across a vast cauldron, I pulled myself out of the dream and opened my eyes to darkness. The last vestige of my dream remained with me, and I could swear I heard my mother's voice calling out to me. Adelaide said something like, "use the lotion!" or was it, "moose in motion?" I didn't know if I really heard her voice, or if it was wishful thinking on my part.

Looking over at my alarm clock, I realized I'd only been asleep for two hours.

"Ugh. This is ridiculous. I need to *do* something!"

Wicked, who'd been happily snoring away on the pillow next to mine, opened one eye and considered me. I could tell her eye was open because the moonlight caught her orb just right and it glowed an eerie phosphorus green as it reflected back. Shutting her eye once more, she stretched then rolled over and went back to sleep.

Throwing my covers to one side, I got up and used the facilities, then donned my slippers and peeked in at my aunt and mother who were still and asleep. I wandered to the lower level of my home and paused on the landing when I thought I heard a strange noise. I could hear the clock on the mantle in my formal living room as it made its soft *tick-tock* sound, but that wasn't it. The sound was a soft rustling, like crumbling paper or sealing up a cereal box.

Cereal. Food.

I think I knew who I'd find raiding my kitchen—for that was assuredly the sound of food either being unwrapped or rewrapped—so I proceeded through the rooms to find out if I was correct.

Instead of Pandora stuffing her face with anything and everything to feed her appetite, I found Adriana snacking on a bowl of Fruit Loops.

What? It's food. It makes you, *ahem*, go blue...but it's still food!

"What are you doing here? Did you drive yourself over?"

"No, dummy. I flew my broom. Of course, I drove."

Still grumpy I see.

"Well, why are you here and eating my cereal?"

"Fur."

Oh, that made so much sense...not!

"Fur? What do you mean by that?"

"I went to have a snack in my own home, but when I poured milk in my bowl and added cereal, there was copious amounts of hair floating in it."

"But where did it come...oh, wait. Werewolves."

Adriana made her hand form a gun and did a shooting motion. "Got it in one."

"It's not like they can help it. They're werewolves!"

"They smell like wet dogs."

"They are keeping great-grandpa safe," I argued.

"There is that."

I looked down and saw one of my chairs had been knocked over. I frowned. Picking it up, I sat across from my great-grandmother and asked what had happened to make it tip over.

"I don't know. It was like that when I walked in," she replied.

I scratched my head and shrugged then told her about my dream. Adriana smiled and made all the right noises, but I could tell she was distracted and morose. That is, until I told her about the fading words I'd heard as I woke up from my troubled slumber.

"That's not what Adelaide said!"

"If it was Mom. I..."

"Liliana! Obviously, it was Adelaide! And she was telling you to use the potion! Not notion. Not motion. And certainly not *lotion!* Potion! Adelaide wants us to use the concoction you brewed to draw Charlie to her side. Impel him, release the magic, so he cannot ignore the call. Where did you tuck it, anyway?"

Adriana was right! In my sleep-deprived state, the fogginess prevented me from making the connection. That had to be my mom begging me to use the potion and release the spell. But was it safe to do so?

"I just thought of something. Isn't tomorrow the traditional day mom would slice her hand and let the blood drip around the base of the sweetbriar rose? What happens if she can't perform the ritual because she's trapped in whatever spell has taken hold of her? What happens to my dad?" I wondered aloud, not really expecting Adriana to offer any kind of rejoinder.

"Perhaps he will wither. Who knows if he is even able to be brought back from whatever magical hold Deanna has placed on him? Too much time has gone by. So much darkness is in his soul now."

Whoa! This maudlin attitude had to stop, and now.

"Stop that! What is wrong with you? If you put that negative thought out there it only benefits Deanna and has our success take a step back and her victory becomes much more certain. We can't have that!" I scolded my great-grandmother who closed her eyes and sighed.

"You're right."

"Come again?" I asked, not quite sure I'd heard her correctly.

"You heard me. I'm not about to repeat it."

Ah ha!

"You stated I was right. As in correct. As in I know what I'm saying, and *you* agree with me."

"Don't get all cocky with me, squirt. It's not like you have a great track record. But on this, you are correct, yes."

Well, then.

I heard another rustling sound, this time coming from my walk-in pantry, and I looked at my great-grandmother in alarm. She raised her eyebrows and wiggled them at me, to show she heard the noise as well.

"Did you go in there to get that cereal?" I whispered.

"No. You left in on the counter with two bowls and spoons out, so I thought you'd forgot to eat it and went to bed."

Two bowls?

Suddenly I heard a muffled cry, and the pantry door flew open, with Pandora and Steve tumbling out and landing hard on the kitchen floor.

"Dorie! Stevie! What are you..." Oh, they did not! I looked at the disheveled state of their clothing and the hot pink lipstick smeared all over Steve's face. Then I took in the fact that Adriana snuck in and probably startled the duo who'd chosen my pantry to hide in, and I realized just exactly what kind of cooking Pandora had been doing.

"Pandora! Please do not tell me you two had sex in my pantry! I'm going to have to throw out all of my food if you did!"

Pandora looked scandalized, which I hadn't expected, and Steve looked abashed.

"Of course we didn't do it in your pantry! What kind of sickos would do something like that?" she cried.

"Well, something was going on! Look at the two of you!"

"We did nothing untoward in that pantry. I promise." Dorie kept looking at Adriana who shrugged and continued to dig into her bowl of cereal with renewed gusto.

"Well, if you didn't, where did you...oh *nooooo!* You didn't?!"

Thinking of the condition the kitchen was in and how I'd found my chair, I came to the same conclusion at precisely the same time as Adriana who shouted, "You had sex on this table?"

"Oopsie!"

I'm going to kill them both.

CHAPTER 12

After spending the next hour scrubbing my table and sanitizing everything in sight, I finally got around to addressing where the vial of potion I'd made was hidden. I sent Pandora off with Steve telling them both I better not catch them ever doing anything even remotely similar in my Uncle Stephen's café or they'd both be dead to me! Especially since Steve Junior arrives in the wee hours of the morning to start the baking for the day!

I was sipping coffee—I scrubbed the pot, my mug, and even opened a new bag of coffee beans as an extra precaution—and the java was soothing my frazzled nerves.

"I thought the little brick hiding place we'd discovered was as good a hiding place as any, so it's been there all this time," I informed Adriana, who was nodding her head in approval.

"We have a problem, however." My great-grandmother took a sip of her coffee then set her mug down and faced me. "The last time you tried using it, the magic had that squishy thing..."

"The koosh ball," I interjected.

"Whatever you call it." Adriana waved her hand in the air, dismissing my explanation. "It made that tiny ball bounce around here and chase Wicked, who we now know was the host for Adelaide. You also left her hair out of the equation. I don't think we should use this brew. I think we add a hair from each of their heads and craft a new one."

I didn't think of that. Adriana was correct—we wanted the strongest potion possible to force our hand and impel Charles Sweet to answer the call—to find his heart's desire.

Placing my mug down on a side table, I ran to my office and grabbed the box that held the items I'd found, including the woven strands of hair that belonged to my mom and dad. Before I left the room, I reached up on the top shelf and hooked the tiny cauldron I'd bought at June's Emporium and rushed back into the den. Setting everything down on the coffee table, I turned to Adriana and offered her the chance to brew the potion.

"You are the stronger witch after all."

"Nonsense, Liliana Sweet! After all these months, and the fact you learned decades of dark magic in a few weeks, you still question your worth? You are strong, stronger even than I am, stronger than Lucretia—or do you think besting her was a fluke? If anyone should brew the potion that will bring Charlie home to Adelaide, it's you."

Wow. I felt my eyes mist and the thump in my throat was pronounced. Deep inside, I knew my great-grandmother's words were true. It's just that, after years of feeling inadequate, alone, and awkward, to have come to this moment was surreal. I turned to face her and took her hands in mine—Adriana's still strong but with a few age spots the only hint of the frailty of age, and mine an exact mirror of what hers must have looked like in her youth.

"You have the right of it. I can do this. I should do it

and bring my parents back together again. Their love resulted in me being here after all and I owe them."

I picked up the recipe I'd written down with the aid of the Winters Sisters, Hermione, and Hortense, making sure I didn't burn my eyebrows off in the interim of my early spell-making attempts and began to read.

"You know? This first attempt did the trick, but one item we chose to omit since the Winters suspected I might not want to involve you or great-grandpa at the time was *hereditary blood elixir.* What is meant by that?" I asked.

"And why didn't you tell me this when you brewed the potion? No wonder it went astray and chased the cat around!" Adriana ran an exasperated hand through her white hair.

"What? Did we do something wrong? Hermione said it wasn't that important..."

"Not important? It's absolutely important! We needed the blood of a male, in this case anyway, an ancestor of Charlie's to ground him and force him to stay the path until he reached Adelaide's side. The blood of an ancient male relative is imperative for this spell to work exactly like we want it to."

"Well, where are we going to find an ancient male ancestor? Oh! Wait! Great-grandpa! He can..."

Adriana began shaking her head forcefully and put her hand up, palm out, to stop any further discussion.

"No. Antonio isn't ancient enough. He is only removed from Charles by two generations. We need someone much older than that to have this magic be as potent as it can be. We need someone further back in our lineage," Adriana explained.

That's great. What were we supposed to do? Dig up a dead relative and hope we could squeeze some DNA out of the corpse to get enough for some dark spells? I shuddered a little and felt sick even contemplating this.

"And how do we manage that? Where are we going to find an ancestor we can take blood from?"

"One will be showing up tomorrow," Adriana glanced at my clock and chuckled. "Let me correct myself. He will be showing up today, well, tonight anyway! The plane touches down at Hartsfield around 4:00 pm, and it will take them about two hours to get here between baggage and traffic," Adriana added with another wiggle of her brows then went back to her coffee.

"Are you going to tell me of whom you are speaking, or do I just give up and wait for the insanity to set in and render me useless? Unless you plan on selling tickets to watch the crazy girl that shoots purple out of her fingertips!"

"I received a phone call earlier when I arrived home from our little hiking expedition. It was decided at the last minute that a delegation was not necessary to deal with this threat and provide the aid we did not request. The Romanos in Italy felt we needed a specialist. So instead, they are sending a much smaller contingency led by Antonio's cousin, Rudy, who is supposed to be a master assassin, or master in the arcane. Honestly? They didn't tell me what he is a specialist in, but I could hear the reverence in their voices when they spoke of his abilities and the sheer magnitude of his personality. He arrives tonight...and we can use his blood."

I felt a migraine coming on and the earlier fogginess came back with a vengeance. Perhaps the information was getting through to my addled brain, or perhaps I didn't want to meet yet another relative when I was having such a difficult time remembering the names of the ones I've encountered here in Sweet Briar. Either way, the one thing that stood out was why was this guy the superior blood donor over Antonio, who is my dad's grandfather?

"Why is this Rudy a candidate, but Grandpa Antonio isn't?" I asked the question that was troubling me.

"Because Rudy has twenty years on Antonio and if we need ancient hereditary blood, I can think of no other older male witch in our family."

Twenty? But that would mean Rudy Dolce was at least one-hundred-and-fifty years old! Egads!

"Have you ever met the man? What is he like? How can someone so old even travel? I mean, he's taking a plane right? That's how he's getting here? And where will we put him?" I shot up and began to pace back and forth and watched as Adriana raised her eyes to the ceiling and sighed.

"Would you stop this worrying? I met Rudy years and years ago, it must be going on eighty, or...hmm...maybe closer to ninety-five years now. He's a dear friend of my father Luigi and he used to bring me treats when I was a child. I don't remember him except for the bits of flotsam that come to you when you remember such things. I believe he was fond of savoiardi biscotti or perhaps the regina ones. Either way, he always had a treat or two and was always a smiling, happy man."

"Grandmother. How old are you? I've never dared ask. Andrea told me Grandpa Antonio is around one hundred-thirty-six. I don't know if it is something you never ask, but...how old are you?"

Adriana began to laugh softly then it turned into a deep belly laugh the likes I've never heard come from the diminutive woman.

"Liliana. Antonio is one hundred and ten years old. I am one hundred and four. I think Andrea and the rest of the family have been having a bit of fun with you. Now, if you want to talk about old, wait until you meet my parents. Wild horses couldn't stop them from coming, despite what the rest of the Romanos desire. Papa is one hundred-thirty-eight and Mama is a year younger. You are going to love Luigi and Elizabetta. You remind me of them both!"

I could hear the sound of bird call, and the early morning twilight was just discernable through my kitchen curtains as I stared open-mouthed at Adriana. My great-*great*-grandparents were still alive?! And they would be here *tonight?*

I almost yearned for the days I would pass out into oblivion...almost.

CHAPTER 13

Why is no one else running around helping me clean and primp and prepare for this monumental visit? Why? Probably because I was the only one home alone with a comatose mother and a ghost for company.

Edith was trying her best. She kept flapping her hands around and blowing on dusty corners to no avail. Pandora had not returned from her night of passion with Steve Junior, and I think she was laying low since my angry diatribe had me threatening exorcism and worse—reporting her to her boss—not that I remotely knew who that might be or if it held any significance.

Aunt Iona woke up and left with the promise to return once she showered and dealt with a few private matters. I suspect my Uncle Owen was feeling left out with all the time she was spending here and not at home with him.

He'd been tagging along with Doc Holcomb, Dennis Carter, and Old Frank who took Max and Rex into the woods to see if they could sniff out this Alan guy. We were waiting on word from them.

Wicked got in on the fun by getting the zoom-zooms while I was vacuuming and managed to knock my little variegated plant off the counter and onto the floor. This wasn't the first time that cat took out the poor thing, and I had a feeling it would shrivel up and die from the abuse. I scooped the dirt back into the ceramic pot it came in and gave it a bit of water, but I swear it was looking at me with a copious amount of disappointment because I hadn't gotten rid of my cat.

"Edith! Stop doing that! You are driving me nuts! Go sit with my mom if you are looking for something to do. I don't want her alone."

Edith looking crestfallen and swirled out of the room. I felt like a heel. I knew I was overreacting and barking orders, and this last one was uncalled-for. I also knew my attitude came from a bad case of nerves and insecurity. It's not every day one meets their antediluvian great-great-grandparents. I was a basket case!

When I asked Adriana why Antonio seemed much older than she was, I discovered he'd not been well after an attack on the prison back when he was in charge of it. It was a vampire attack, and it was almost deadly. The vampire in question was unstable and had some kind of unnamed disorder, and when he bit—yes, he actually bit—Antonio, he became tainted with a foul magic. If it weren't for that, he'd probably be as spry as Adriana!

As I continued to clean, the weight of my new life bore down on me, and I fought with the thoughts that kept running through my mind. I would live a long, long time if no evil asshat got the better of me. Did I want to though? I mean, everyone hopes to reach one hundred. But just how long would I be walking around this earth and was it something I could accept and deal with?

I deliberated on the three relatives that would arrive—

gulp!—in less than one hour and wondered if my home was adequate enough to accommodate those who were truly ancient and probably needed walkers or even a wheelchair to get around.

"A wheelchair! Oh my gosh! How will they get on the porch? Will the doorframe be wide enough to allow the chair entry? This is a mess! *A mess!*"

"What's a mess?" In walked Lorcan looking like a mechanic version of a GQ model. He had on a skintight dark blue tee and a pair of Levi 501s which showed off his fine behind. But I was too distracted to appreciate any of it. Instead, I did what any twenty-six-year-old dark witch would do when faced with the arrival of visitors from the Old Country.

"Whoa! Lily, sweetheart! Why are you crying?" Lorcan looked askance at my drippy face and sniveling nose. I stopped what I was doing, collapsed on the floor, and began to rock back and forth.

"I can't do this! I am unprepared for this. I am an idiot! A wannabe dark witch. They will see right through me! They will wish for any other great-great-granddaughter but the one they are stuck with! Perhaps they will prefer someone like Nora over me...or Pandora. Or...or..."

"Or they will fall in love with you and all this turmoil is for nothing. Come here, Lily. Jeez, woman! Stop rocking and...no! Don't roll over into a ball, silly!" Lorcan pulled me up from my fetal position and led me to my favorite chair in the den.

"No! I can't sit! I fluffed the pillows! I made the perfect crease! I can't have them come in here and see an uncreased pillow! What will they think?" I screeched. Lorcan jumped back, eyes wide.

"Oh, boy."

"Will you please do something about her? I am losing

my mind over the ruckus she is making!" Edith came floating back into the room and spoke as if Lorcan could hear her. He couldn't. I shot her my darkest scowl which gave away the fact she'd entered the den. Lorcan looked around then sighed.

"Is Edith here?"

I nodded yes.

"Edith, will you please put your differences aside and go find Pandora. I am going to need all the help I can get. See if she can find if Jake and Becky are free as well...Andrea too, and tell them to head over here. We might as well all be present and give my fiancé the support she needs to deal with the Italian delegation!"

Edith saluted and left. Since Lorcan couldn't see her either, I informed him that she'd acquiesced, leaving to fetch the others.

"I need a tape measure."

Lorcan gave me a puzzled glance then wandered into my mudroom to search for one. That's what I loved about this man. No questioning. No demanding I tell him why I needed something or trying to talk me out of an idea or thought. He just shrugged and found me what I needed every time. This time was no different because he came back in moments later carrying a retractable tape measure that Bud forgot here during the renovation a few months back, and I forgot to give back to him when he was just here fixing the window.

"Do you have any idea how wide my doors need to be to accommodate a wheelchair?" I sniffed, wiping my nose with my arm. I know, but I wasn't thinking straight, and my arm worked.

"Wheelchair? Why do you..."

Seeing that asking me that one question had my chin quivering again, Lorcan held up his hands. "You know what? I'm not sure, but I will measure your doors—all of them—and then we can Google what the standard width is, and then check out what any larger one's dimensions are. How's that?"

I gave Lorcan a watery smile then went to my kitchen table and sat—no pillows to besmirch, so I could.

I laid my head down on the table then turned my neck sideways so I could watch Lorcan at work measuring the back door. He did have a fine behind, and those jeans put naughty ideas in my head. Then I remembered what Pandora and Steve had done on this very table and I shot upright again.

"I need more bleach."

"OK. I will pick some up."

"I need it now, Lorcan."

"Baby. I thought you needed me to measure the...um, OK. I will be right back." Lorcan flew out the back door to his truck which I heard turn over, tires spinning gravel in his attempt to hurry and make everything better in my world.

I knew I was acting like an insane woman, but I couldn't help it. What if my great-great-grandparents really did hate me? It could happen! I'd like to think I was a charming, loveable, witch and the light and life of this family. I'd like to think that, however, a little voice in my mind always whispered "what ifs" leaving me in doubt that anyone in my family could tolerate me, let alone love me. Issues much, Lily?

I shot up and rushed into the mudroom, dragging the bucket and mop out with a bottle of Spic-N-Span, and began to mop the sunroom floor. I had to do something or I'd start pulling my hair out. After that task was accomplished, I moved into the den. The floors in there were slate but had comfy rugs strategically placed hither and yon which I moved out of the way by draping them over the sofa. That finished, I went to clean the half bath off the kitchen.

I glanced in the mirror and almost jumped back when my eyes landed on my reflection. I looked haunted and crazed. I pinched my cheeks and tried smiling. Whoa! Yeah, not a good idea. I gave off the impression I'd just escaped from the mental ward.

"Hey, kitty, where's your momma? I have news."

I heard Pandora and returned to the kitchen only to morph into a screaming banshee, complete with spittle flying out of my mouth.

"What are you doing? Both of you? Get off those floors! Get off! Move! I just washed them!"

Pandora and Wicked paused for just a nanosecond before collectively shooting straight up in the air and landing on my sofa. Wicked didn't stop there but shot over to the fireplace mantle and curled up at one end giving me a wide-eyed look that showed me just how far I'd fallen into lunacy and hysteria.

I now knew what they meant when they said, "looney bin." Trust me...I was in it.

I closed myself in my own private box of crazy and threw away the key. And I hate the word hysteria and all the connotations behind it, but right now I gave myself a pass. Because I was definitely hysterical. If I could crawl up into my own uterus and take a nap, I would.

"Oh, sugar! You've got it bad, honey," said Pandora. "You're shaking and quaking like one of those tiny Mexican dog thingies with the bug eyes. Chimichangas or something."

"Chihuahuas. They are called chihuahuas," I stated numbly.

"Either way, they taste the same. So... what are we

going to do about you and these nerves? We can't have you meeting family in this condition. I know! Wine!"

"I haven't whined. I'm not whining!"

Pandora took a tentative step off the sofa, and when I didn't bark at her any longer, she came over to where I stood.

"No, silly. The drink. As in vino. White or red? Have a glass to settle your nerves. It will do wonders."

Just then June Carter came bustling in with a basket on one arm and a bottle of something in the other.

"I brought fresh rolls for dinner and a bottle of wine. I haven't seen Luigi or Elizabetta since I was your age, Lily. It's been too long."

"When was anyone going to inform me they were still among the living? How could y'all forget about something so important?" I asked. And yes, I said "y'all." Now you comprehend just how off my rocker I've fallen that I'd suddenly gone southern in speech.

"Here. Give me that." Pandora reached for the bottle and before we could stop her, she had the cork out and had poured me a glass. "Drink."

Well, I think she said drink. She still had the cork in her mouth and began chewing it. Wait. How did she...? Never mind.

I downed it in one shot and poured another. June looked on wide-eyed then said, "I think I should go get a few more bottles," then left.

"I have to prepare dinner. Oh, my gosh. No one is here and I have to prepare dinner for an army!"

"Lily! Stop. Use your magic. No one is going to chastise you for cheating. Heck, I won't tell anyone if you won't. And I'm certain June would keep your secret—she's like another mother to you."

Could I do such a thing? Would I be able to pull it off?

I'd never tried conjuring an entire meal. In the early days of my studies, I managed to light a candle or two only to have it backfire and cause a small emergency. An entire meal would be a monumental task. However, I knew how to do it. I had the ability.

"I just have to have leftovers to pull off that sort of magic, right?" I asked Dorie who nodded yes.

"OK, I'm in. Do me a favor, will you? Run to Joe's and get me his stuffed cannelloni, a small side salad, and his chicken marsala. Here, pay with this. Then rush home. I will duplicate the meals and be all set! Dorie, you are amazing!" Before I knew what I was doing, I threw my arms around the crossroads demon and shocked us both. Separating, we laughed nervously, then Dorie returned my hug once more.

"I got ya, kid." And with that, she was off and running.

CHAPTER 14

"Gesù Cristo. Liliana è ubriaca!"

Grandpa Antonio took one look at me and uttered those dire words. I was *not* drunk, and Jesus had nothing to do with it.

"Why is she grinning like that? No, seriously. Look at her! It's like the Joker got to her or something," said Andrea and started scratching her elbows.

I found this remarkably funny and began to chuckle. Then I burped and threw my head back to guffaw loudly.

"Lorcan Reid! Why didn't you stop her from imbuing so much wine! Quick, someone make coffee! Adriana will be here with the Italians in about twenty minutes," Uncle Stephen scolded, shaking his head at the gravity of my condition.

I felt fine.

"I went to get bleach but then Sheriff Buford called asking me to meet him at the shop. When I arrived, he and Tiff were waiting with Keisha Holcomb's Subaru on a tow truck. They found it near the parking area near the Coleman River where everyone goes fishing. Doc Holcomb is heading that way with Owen, Dennis, and Frank as we speak to see if the hellhounds can pick up a trail. I secured the vehicle in my shop and Glen left, but Tiff needed my help with Lucifer again, and I had to do that before I returned here with the bleach. It kind of took a lot longer than I thought it would," he said sheepishly.

I squinted.

I may have growled a little.

"Plus, June was the one who brought two cases of wine! What were you thinking?"

After Lorcan deflected the blame to poor June, who was wringing her hands looking miserable, I decided I needed to step in and set things straight.

"I nom dung and noo blam Joo." There. That should clear things up.

"Did she just say she isn't drunk? Seriously? Look at her. She is swaying back and forth." Jake was watching me warily, as if I might suddenly get sick all over his Armani suit. He had a thing for Armani. Becky kept rubbing his arm and making sympathetic noises. I just wasn't certain if they were for my benefit or Jake's.

"And where is Pandora? I don't understand how dinner could be this far along and everything is spotless and put away without her helping Lily with the cleanup and such," Lorcan added for good measure.

I swirled in his direction and pointed my finger at his nose. "Ooo nude be ashay duv ooo sef! Tee-funny dis, Tee-funny dat! Hmph."

I watched my finger wiggle in Lorcan's face then turned it around and did the same in front of my nose. How fascinating. I smiled at the tip of my digit then burped. "Oopsie!" I suddenly found everything hilarious and began to slow dance around the room to Vivaldi.

"What is she doing now? Where is that coffee?!

Adriana and my mom are going to walk in with our family and Lily is in no condition to meet them!" Andrea cried.

"Here it is," said June, placing a mug in my hand and spotting it lest I do something foolish like toss it in Lorcan's face. Hey! That's not a bad idea.

"Lily, please stop moving around and sit. Drink up." June led me to the kitchen table and tried to get me to settle down.

"Noooo....Vivadee! Vivadee...I dance!"

"Viva...what? Lily, there is no music playing. Especially not Vivaldi!" Andrea let out a snort.

That's what *she* thinks. I could hear it loud and clear.

Suddenly, I didn't feel so good.

"I tink I nee to uck up." The room became deathly silent, and I watched everyone reacting to my words—some trying to figure out what I meant and others looking shocked.

"Upchuck! She means upchuck! Lily needs to hurl. Move it." Andrea rushed over to me and gently led me through the dining room and living room into my front foyer and up the stairs to my bedroom. I just reached the threshold when I heard cries and exclamations from below and knew my great-great-grandparents had just arrived with Rudy. Adriana and Chiara made good time.

Time. *Time.* Yeah, I think it was time for me to nap.

"Oh, Lily."

Looking down at my feet, I became confused a moment then realized I must have let the wine come back up. Why did I do that? What a waste of good vino!

"I've got this." Pandora flew into the room and pushed Andrea out of the way, shooing her out and back downstairs to my guests. "Stall them. Give me fifteen minutes..."

"Buuurp!"

".... maybe twenty. And I will have her as good as new! Darn it, Lily! I was gone for thirty minutes. How did you manage to get yourself in so much trouble?"

"Een vino vertooz!" I giggled. Then Dorie placed her hand on my forehead, and I went to a different place. A place far, *far* away...

❧

"OH, GOD. I'M DYING."

"You're not dying."

"Well, I want to die. Can you help? You can have my soul and everything."

"Don't ever offer me that, sugar. Those words are like an elixir in my brain, OK?" Pandora was brushing my hair and putting it in an updo. She'd showered with me—and how embarrassing was that?—then got me into clothing of her choice and began to work on my face and hair.

"They are stalling. Everyone is enjoying hors d'oeuvres and wine. They think you have just prepared the grand feast and needed to freshen up."

"Ugh...please don't mention wine. I never want to see wine again."

"You're just lucky I thought to head back to Joe's and get some tidbits. I had a feeling the meal would be delayed a bit, and look, I'm right," Dorie said.

"I have the food on warming platters, right? The rolls are on the table? Did we remember the napkins?" I asked, worry starting me to agonize once more.

"Stop it! Everything is perfect. You are just lucky I have stronger magic than you witches. Once one of you gets that drunk, no manner of witch magic can reverse it and you are just as bad as a human—worse even!"

"Dorie? Can I ask you about something? Can you tell me how we are related? I know we don't have the time what with..."

"No. It's OK. We have a bit of time. I need to get your makeup on and let your hair settle. We aren't related in the way you think. It's not as if a demon ancestor of mine got busy with a witch relation of yours and made babies," Pandora stated.

I watched as she selected the color palette she'd paint my face with and hoped I wouldn't come out looking like a harlot—or worse, a clown!

"My blood entered your system when I saved Antonio's life."

What? What did Pandora mean by that? Oh! "You saved him when he got attacked by the vampire?" I asked.

"Adriana told you about that?" she asked, and I nodded yes. "Yeah. I was there. He'd lost so much blood and the vamp transferred his toxins into Antonio so fast, I had no choice. I had to give him some of mine or he would have died. Once demon blood gets in you, it's there to stay and will affect your offspring. Your Aunt Chiara and father Charles have demon blood in them, and it passed down to you. If you and lover boy have children, it will be in them as well."

Interesting.

"Will I? I mean, does it change me somehow?"

"If you are worried about moving on to your just rewards or suddenly morphing into a crossroads demon and nabbing souls at moonlight, relax, sugar. It's in you, but it doesn't make you a card-carrying imp."

I relaxed when her words registered, but then she ruined the calm by continuing, "However, no one knows what having siren magic mixed in will do. That came from

Adelaide and passed to you through her. Chiara and Charles have nothing to do with any siren blood. So you are an anomaly. Who knows? You just might sprout some horns and start roasting your victims like marshmallows. It should be interesting, anyway!"

CHAPTER 15

Heading downstairs after that little revelation had me trembling again, but my nervousness didn't have the chance to last long upon meeting the Italian brigade. I fully expected to find aged and bent gnome-like grandparents and a semi-gnome-like cousin. Instead, I stopped short and felt my mouth drop into an 'O' when my eyes landed on my newest family members.

Rudy was tall. Like vampire tall. Easily the upper sixes if not touching seven feet. He was rail thin and dashing and could not possibly be in his one hundreds. Yet I knew he was. But that wasn't what shocked me and rendered me speechless. Luigi and Elizabetta Romano were nothing like what I'd expected. Instead of bent and crooked, they were ramrod straight like Adriana. Instead of frail and in wheelchairs, they wore tracksuits with the Italian flag emblazoned on the back and wore sneakers that looked like they'd gotten major usage. In other words, those two 'old' people were in better shape than their great-great-granddaughter!

What's more, I wasn't prepared for their accents.

"Lily, darling girl. Come here and give me a hug you sweet thang! Look at her Lou! She's a button, I tell ya. A button!"

"She's a toots alright! Come here, sweetheart. Give your old grandpappy a kiss!"

Whoa.

Then it dawned on me. These two might be Italian and all, but Marcus, Luigi's father, was the one who'd emigrated to the United States. Luigi was born here. Elizabetta too, from other transplanted Italians. They were Americans living abroad! How could I forget?

After much kissing and fawning upon, I was encased in a hug from Uncle Rudy. "Oh, such a babester! Look at you! My word but you look like Annie! Doll baby...she is the spitting image of you!" This he addressed to Adriana with a slight lisp and flip of his hair. I remained transfixed on his polished fingernails and... was that eyeliner? It was! Uncle Rudy was wearing makeup. And it looked better on him than it did me! No, seriously. The man was gorgeous. He made Brian Chase look like a puny punk all wet behind the ears.

And those eyes! Women around the world would kill for his lashes! They were two turquoise orbs of wonder that I found myself lost in.

Rudy's hair looked black, but it was the darkest shade of red I'd ever seen on a person. It reminded me of the old movie star, Ava Gardner's color—it was perfection! His cheekbones were unquestionably chiseled by the gods and his smile would no doubt stop traffic at rush hour in Manhattan.

It was with certainty I'd decided he batted for the same team and wondered how many women's hearts he broke when they couldn't sway him to their side. He must have a trail of them lining his front walk, their tears the water for his lawn!

I barely grabbed a bit of the hors d'oeuvres when Pandora and Andrea entered the dining room laden with platters of food. June was helping. They refused to let me do a thing and I found myself sandwiched between Luigi and Elizabetta—who I discovered preferred I call them Lou and Lizzie—with Rudy across from me.

"I mean really! Once you get to our age, adding all those greats become monotonous! Lou and Lizzie will do. Plus, it makes us feel younger! Right, Chiara? Your aunt has a difficult time of it, refuses to call me Lizzie! Such nonsense."

"You could call me 'hey you,' and I'd answer. Right, honey?" Lou gave me a wink and I giggled. What on earth was I ever worried about? I felt like such a fool!

Grandpa Antonio was on the other side of the table and raised his glass of wine in salute. "Ma, you look much better now, Liliana. Tutti bene!"

"Well, this food certainly looks good. I wonder why I can't smell anything though?" Adriana looked at her plate in confusion.

"Mine smells like heaven!" Lorcan said, taking a bite and sighing in satisfaction.

"Mine too," said June. She skipped the cannelloni and went right for the marsala. I felt a prickle of worry beginning and it blossomed into all-out panic when Adriana grimaced and spit her mouthful back onto her plate.

"What is this?" she asked.

"Dinner?" I tried for brevity, but Adriana was having nothing of it.

"Liliana. Did you make this dinner, or did you conjure it?" she demanded.

I glanced at Pandora who shook her head and

shrugged then took a bite of food, only to roll her eyes to the heavens. Odd for a demon!

"Um...I kind of cheated?" I said guiltily.

"Hold up before you start yelling at her! It was my idea," said Dorie.

"Let me guess. Joe? You bought two different dinners and conjured our meal from them?" Adriana asked.

"Yes," I said in a quiet voice.

"Liliana. You might be a great dark witch in the making, but please stay out of the kitchen when it comes to duplicating a meal. All you did was look at what you wanted to create but failed to add the scent and taste. This tastes like an old shoe!"

"Hey! That's OK, honey! I like old shoes," said Lou.

Groan.

Crud on a cracker! What have I done?

AFTER A RUSHED ORDER of pizza and salads, and a few tales of days gone by, we congregated in my den sipping coffee and eating cannoli—Aunt Chiara and Uncle Stephen ran to the café and raided the cooler—and we were now discussing Adelaide and how to go about getting Charlie freed from the clutches of Deanna.

Uncle Owen showed up with information on the hellhounds. They'd apparently picked up the trail of this Alan dude when they took the beasts to the fairgrounds after everyone had left for the day. They only had to erase five memories from folks who happened by and freaked at the sight of the massive hounds. The trail ran cold on the other side of the high school, but the dogs indicated they wanted to run up the road which means the guy probably had a vehicle parked there and left the area in it. That was an error on his part because the schools had so many cameras everywhere pointing in all directions all we had to do was contact Brian Chase and have him pull the feed. Owen had already called him. By tomorrow we should know what make and model vehicle Alan drove, and the hunt would be on in full force. They also picked something up at the Coleman River where Keisha's car was found, so there is that.

"How long has Adelaide been out of it this time?" Lizzie asked. For some reason, it was easy for me to think of the elderly duo as Lou and Lizzie. Go figure?

"It's only been two days now. Tomorrow will be day three. We are all mystified by this turn of events. Even the clerics have no idea," Adriana said.

I still worried about the fact that today was the day my mother usually gave her blood sacrifice for my father. I wondered what if anything would happen when we reached midnight. Would he be OK?

I jumped up and opened the drawer in the table by my fireplace and removed the little poppet doll that represented Charlie Sweet. Bringing it to my great-great-grandparents and Uncle Rudy, I relayed the story behind it and how it had been planted under the sweetbriar rose bush, and how Adelaide, inside Wicked, had protected the shrub with her life.

"Oh! But that's incredible! How could you not realize the importance of this revelation? Adriana, I'm surprised at you! You, of all people, should have known what this meant. Lily is the Sweet Briar Witch! We have known since you informed me of the deceit Adelaide and Charlie perpetrated, that Lily is the product of two dark witches, and has siren blood from Addy and demon blood from Charlie. You forget...she also has a modicum of shifter blood from us—well, the Romanos anyway. She is the Sweet Briar Witch!" Lizzie proclaimed.

What the heck did that mean?

"Don't forget vampire. Lily has vampire blood in her," Pandora offered.

The room exploded with denials and outrage.

"Lily has no vampire blood! How can you suggest such a thing? Not that I have anything against vampires per se—after all, I adore Mortimer—but we have no known vampires on either side of the family. Where did you come up with such nonsense, Pandora?" scolded Adriana. "And don't say it's because Lucretia became one. That was something she did on her own. It's not like she passed anything down to us. Wait! Vampires cannot procreate! They can only..."

"They do thees by bite. Ma, Adriana, il mio amore, I became so when I attacked. I pass thees to my great-granddaughter," Antonio stated quietly.

"What are you talking about Tony? You're not... you can't be. How?" Adriana looked so distressed I worried about her health.

Pandora stood and walked over to Grandpa Antonio and placed a hand on his shoulder.

"Let me explain." Dorie went on to tell everyone present the same tale she told me about Antonio being attacked and her magic used to save his life...by giving him demon's blood which he did pass on to his children. What she hadn't informed me was the damage had such a severe effect on Antonio that the only way to prolong his life and give him time for his body to accept the demon blood was to alter the vampire venom injected when he was bitten and let it turn him, effectively making him a vampire.

Antonio proved this by allowing his fangs to extend, giving us a glimpse of a side he chose to hide even from

Adriana who looked ravaged by this news. I stared in fascination and felt a stirring deep inside me that felt alien yet familiar at the same time.

"But that means nothing! You obviously were still able to procreate because your witch blood was dominant. Charlie and I are not vampires! You cannot pass that gene! So why are you two insisting Lily is a vampire?" Aunt Chiara was almost as upset as Adriana. Her eyes were glassy as if she had unshed tears just waiting for the right moment to come spilling out and down her face.

"It's what happened when she was a baby. After Adelaide, Charlie and Jess returned from Las Vegas with baby Lily in tow. I was trapped inside the book and Adelaide used to read tales I would show her to settle the baby and get her sleepy enough to drop off," Pandora explained. "One night, when Antonio came to babysit, Lily was sitting on his lap while I entertained them both with a tale. Remember, even in book form I could talk and rhyme, and did so with abandon that night."

Pandora sat down on the floor at Antonio's feet, tucking her legs to one side.

"Antonio must have drifted off and inadvertently his teeth extended and baby Lily, always difficult to settle down to sleep, reached up to touch them, only she startled Antonio and, in his confusion, managed to embed his fang straight through Lily's tiny hand, right through her palm. Lily screamed with pain. You have to remember, when a vampire bites with the intent to turn you, it can be an almost seductive and pleasurable sensation. But an accidental bite—or one intending to do harm—feels like an icy-hot dagger, as sharp as a razor and a hundred times more intense coursing through your body so severely, you gladly beg for death to rid yourself of the pain."

Dorie looked at me sadly, and I noticed Grandpa Antonio crying.

"You can imagine how much pain Lily felt. Antonio was frozen, unable to come up with a way to heal the baby and remove the excruciating agony she was experiencing. So I began to chant in a singsong voice that mesmerized him and lulled him to do the only thing I could think of that would heal her wounds and removed the venom spreading through her veins like rapid fire. I put the suggestion in Antonio's mind that he needed to heal Lily's wound with his saliva, then offer her his own blood to strengthen her enough to nullify the vampire's cursed blood that was now part of her and would forever be part of her. Antonio turned Lily that night. That very instant. She went from a wailing babe, desperate to free herself from the pain and agony to a content little vampire youngling in mere minutes—even if she was a crossbreed."

"Crossbreed? Lily isn't a crossbreed—she's a Heinz 57 at this point! Just how many more paranormal beings does she have in her blood? What kind of Breed is she?" cried June. "What's more, when the Elders find out, what will they do to her?"

I'd like to say that was the most momentous occurrence of the evening. But just then we heard a shuffling sound coming from the formal rooms, and an obviously spelled Adelaide came waltzing into the kitchen, turned to the mudroom, and went outside to perform her ritual.

We all managed to reach her side just as she sliced her palm letting the blood flow into the ground surrounding the sweetbriar rose bush.

CHAPTER 16

I spent the rest of the night staring at myself in my bathroom mirror trying to get my fangs to punch out. It never happened. I wound up falling asleep next to my mom who returned to her bed and fell back into a fitful slumber.

Wicked joined us and we made an odd trio, but at least I managed to drop off—and didn't dream at all—not that I could remember anyway.

Antonio, shamed and heartbroken, went home with Adriana—the Italian delegation going with them to stay in their roomy Victorian. I hoped Antonio and Adriana could work out the miles of hurt as a result of him keeping the truth from her all these years, not trusting to share such a momentous secret with her, and they would not let this become an issue between them.

Poor Grandpa Antonio. I didn't blame him at all. I didn't even try and lay the blame on Pandora for suggesting the only remedy she could come up with, so little time did they have to heal me before I became forever damaged by the deranged vampire's bite.

Lorcan gave me the longest hug before he departed, trying to infuse me with as much of his soothing empath healing as he could muster. I couldn't look him in the eyes, however despite his trying to get me to look in his. I just couldn't. Not yet. I felt like such a freak.

No.

I *am* a freak.

I could tell a subtle shift in the atmosphere signaled that everyone in my family felt the same. I mean, it's one thing to have two different Breed in your bloodline. Things happened. Witches fell for shifters or what have you. I get it. But I'm something so wrong, so outlandish, with so many unknowns as to what it all meant, that I think my days as the prodigal daughter, beloved and welcome, were over.

And I couldn't blame anyone for feeling this way.

I wanted to jump out of my skin and run for the hills.

I felt fissure course through me and knew I was being watched. Slowly opening my eyes to notice it was now morning, the sun gave ample light with which to see. I found myself staring into the open eyes of my mother.

"Lily. Save Charlie. He's dying. Call him to me. Today." Adelaide barely got the last of her words out when her eyes rolled back in her head, and she passed out cold. I shot out of bed but ordered Wicked to stand guard and flew out of the room to find Pandora and call Adriana. We needed Uncle Rudy here pronto—and we needed to create that potion within the hour if possible.

I wouldn't hear another word otherwise.

It was time to call Charlie Sweet home.

"ADD a pinch more of the wormwood. Not that much, just a sliver. That's good...very good Lily. OK...now the liquid. Mix it in your cauldron but don't pour it in all at once. Dribble it in until it just covers the wormwood, then add the strands of hair, four of Charlie's and four of Adelaide's." Uncle Rudy was instructing me on the proper way to create the potion and I could tell even Adriana was impressed. The man knew his stuff!

"OK, now for the best part. My blood. I will add exactly four drops and then we wait and see if it is accepted."

I winced when Rudy jabbed a needle into his thumb although he didn't react in the slightest. It wasn't that I was squeamish or feared pain, but it recalled the story Pandora told us and I could picture Antonio's fang plunging into my palm and felt the phantom ache even though I never knew it occurred—or couldn't remember.

"Now remember. The last time you crafted this you made the intent behind it to find Charlie's heart's desire to test the magic. You said your koosh ball slammed into Wicked who had Adelaide locked away inside her. This time, I've added ingredients that subtly change our intent but with outstanding results—we hope. This time, with the urgency behind Adelaide's condition and the sweetbriar rose being tied to Charlie's well-being, we are making a superfast working elixir that should whisk your dad here almost instantaneously. Or we hope anyway. My blood is strong however—so our odds are good."

"What do you think is wrong with my mom?" I wondered if Rudy would have an opinion or a theory.

"I think she is under a self-imposed sleep spell that enables her to commune with Charlie in spirit. I've seen something like it before, a very long time ago. With Adelaide under as she is, her subconscious can tap into the tether she shares with her soul mate—your father. One hopes she can whisper to him and in some way, her words can reach him."

I liked the sound of that and hoped Rudy was correct.

The sound of sizzling and bubbling came from my little cauldron, and I watched as the magic swirled and blended turning the mishmash of colors and textures into an amber liquid. This was fascinating. Crafting a potion has quickly become one of my favorite things about being magical. I certainly did better with potions than trying to conjure a meal!

"I think it worked," I said, sitting back at peering up at Rudy.

"Indeed," he replied.

"Is it finished?" I asked.

"No, we have a few more ingredients to add and... oh! But we've made a grave mistake! Unless you can find another siren tear, we will have to use some of the old potion in this new one. Unorthodox, to be sure! But what choice do we have? Also, the chant. Let me see it again."

I handed my Uncle Rudy the handwritten spell Hermione helped me with the first time I attempted to call my father home.

Charlie Sweet was sitting in a tree
True love's waiting; come find me!
Over the hill or underground
Wherever she's been, she must be found
Find her Charlie listen to my voice
Return to Sweet Briar; you have no choice!

"OH, no, no. This is pedestrian. It's too predictable and cute. We need The Book of Lovers Lost to come up with something with more hubris. More weight. The intensity must be extreme and compelling!" Rudy insisted.

"And just where do we get that?" I was almost afraid of the answer and groaned when Ariana piped up. She'd been sitting quietly, not getting involved in the spellcasting, seemingly introspective and sullen. I figured she had a lot on her plate right now dealing with the revelations of the previous day. But now she became animated and responded to my query.

It's in the Forbidden Library, dummy. Where else would it be?"

Oh, no. Not again. No way!

"I am not..."

"No, you are not going to have to go down there to retrieve it."

"Because I'm... wait. What?" I was confused.

"Liliana. We don't need you to retrieve the book. Let me call Susanne and get things moving. Your time would be better served heading to Nichols Pond to see if Tarni Vanderzee has left or is still there. A fresh tear is better than an old potion. By the time you get back, Susanne should be here with our magical tome." Adriana finished, nodding for emphasis.

Well, OK then!

Susanne Washington was my great-grandmother's best friend, Keeper of Tomes of the Forbidden Library, and she was one of two people with the key, the other being Jerry, my fairy godfather—a long story if there ever was one! She was also a minor witch and a card-carrying member of her Methodist Church—she even sang in the choir. She was also Doc Holcomb's aunt and Keisha's great aunt. I knew she must be beyond distracted with the disappearance of the young woman and Grandpa Antonio's nurse.

"I think Tarni will smack me if I come at her with another request. But I will try. I just hope she's still there. I got the impression last time that she'd departed and is off on a journey to her past. The sense of loss and sorrow was profound when we bade our farewells to each other...this might be a lesson in futility."

"Be that as it may, we need a tear, and she's a siren. Go try and find her. We will meet you back here in an hour or so, and take Pandora with you," ordered Adriana.

TEN MINUTES LATER, I was in my Jeep with Pandora and Wicked—the latter refusing to stay home like any normal cat but was instead laying across my dashboard in the sun. On her back, all four paws in the air as she stretched her full length—she was such an oddball.

Dorie was driving me insane flipping through my radio channels and stuffing her face. We were barely out of my driveway, and she'd already discovered and consumed my stash of black jellybeans Lorcan kept me flush with, when she began to whine about being so hungry...

"I can eat a farmer's shorts through a tennis racket!"

Ugh. Really?

Sweet Briar had zero fast food joints in keeping with our folksy charming mien, so that meant Joe's Diner, Uncle Stephen's café, otherwise known as Enchanté Café, or one of the other various restaurants sprinkled around town. Pandora wanted subs—roast beef, specifically, and since we were heading in the direction of the French bistro which also had a European-style deli on one side, we opted to stop there to get her a meal—or ten.

I pleaded with Dorie to remain in my Jeep, but she wasn't having any of it. "How will I know what to get?"

"You said you wanted roast beef! I think I can handle it from here."

"That was merely a suggestion. Look at this place! The smells coming out of it remind me of standing outside Davoli on the Rue Cler in Paris! I need to take a gastronomical tour before I decide on something!"

"Davoli?"

"It's an amazing Italian deli—well, they have a bit of everything from all over Europe, but the family is generations deep in Paris, and Italian. It's one of my favorite haunts when I'm in the City of Lights. We should go sometime," suggested Pandora.

"Yeah, I dropped a fortune on my home and buying this vehicle. Paris might be a while out in the affordability department," I answered drolly.

"Nonsense! I have an apartment across the street. Although I have no idea its condition since I've been away so long. I let a vampire friend squat there, and you know how long they like to sleep. Perhaps she is still there in slumber... who knows?" said Pandora.

Having lived in poverty my entire life, this newfound semi-wealth with income coming in from my art but the trust my family set up for me as well, didn't do enough to drive away the constant fear that I'd wake up someday broke, homeless, and hungry. It eased up as the weeks went by, but it was still there, in the far recesses of my mind, and I couldn't shake it—and probably never will.

A trip to Paris would be incredible, however.

This moment of reverie left me standing beside my Jeep and I didn't notice I'd lost Pandora who was even now running wild in the bistro. *Uh oh.* I went to warn Wicked not to leave her spot on the dashboard, but she too had departed, leaving a sinking feeling in the pit of my stomach.

Oh, no... just how bad is this going to be?

I could feel the sweat trickling down my neck, my shirt already sticking to my body. June in Georgia could be pleasantly mild, or the humidity could kill you in an instant. Today was one of those humid days, and I was feeling it. Hurrying into the bistro, I expected to find bedlam, but instead, Dorie was having a lively chat with the man behind the counter.

"I do indeed adore escargots! I cannot believe you carry Saveurs!"

Peering around surreptitiously, hoping to find out where Wicked had gotten herself to, I breathed a sigh of relief when I didn't spy her furry body anywhere in the shop. Perhaps she jumped out of my Jeep and was even now on her way back home. One could hope anyway.

"Oh, definitely. I used to stay at the George V all the time but then I nabbed this cute little apartment of my own. I was telling Lily here, it's just across the street diagonally from..."

"Um, Dorie? I hate to interrupt, but we are kind of on a time restriction here. Shouldn't you order something to eat?"

I received a double set of frowns from Pandora and who I assumed was the owner or manager of the bistro, so I zipped it and sighed internally.

"I guess you have a point. OK, Philippe. I'd love a roast beef on brioche and please add the rémoulade spread you mentioned. Then I'll take some escargots in the red wine. Oh! And some pears with brie and prosciutto di Parma! And a baguette! And some macarons—just the rose lychee, the vanilla bourbon, and the pistachio. And..."

"Dorie!"

"...and I guess that's it." Pandora looked a bit crestfallen that she wouldn't get to eat out the entire restaurant, but I had pressing matters to attend to—her gastronomic tour of European delicacies could wait for another day.

I paid for Dorie's vittles—another thing we'd have to discuss since I didn't know if crossroads demons earned an income, but I wasn't about to continue supporting her gluttonous habits. Paris apartment or no!

We were about to leave the bistro when I hear a commotion coming from the back kitchen. Suddenly a tiny man in a chef toque came running out the swinging doors wielding a huge rolling pin and chasing Wicked who had a chocolate croissant in her mouth. She was growling. I shouted at the man to stop chasing her—it was a lost cause after all. Pandora was in front of me and opened the door so Wicked could make her escape. I just turned around and left another $20 on the counter. I mean really—did I even have a choice?

CHAPTER 17

"What happened to the pond?" I wailed.

We'd driven from the bistro to Nichols Pond in record time with Pandora consuming everything I'd purchased just as I parked and turned off my vehicle. Wicked gave us a lazy glance and I figured she'd remain behind, sunning herself and settling in for a long nap. Especially since that croissant lasted all of two minutes.

I thought a short walk along the trail and a few minutes calling Tarni in the hopes we'd garner another tear would make for a pleasant afternoon. Nothing could have prepared me for the disaster that was the once pristine waters of the pond I'd come to think of as Tarni's home.

Where the waters were once an incredible and inexplicable turquoise blue, and very opaque, they were now brackish and slimy with algae. The area grasses looked droopy and not lush like I would expect it to be this time of year. No sound of bird calls or woodland creatures reached our ears. Everything was eerily silent and there was sense of expectation like malignant eyes were tracking our approach.

"Tarni? Tarni Vanderzee, it's Lily. Are you here?" I felt foolish yelling at a body of water, but I didn't know how to go about calling the siren any other way.

I didn't think Tarni was anywhere in or around this filthy and pathetic puddle. Dejected, I motioned to Pandora that we should turn and head back the way we'd come, when suddenly we heard a crackling sound almost like fabric ripping but with an electric kick.

Turning back around had me face-to-face with the very woman I've wanted to murder every night since it was revealed she was the main reason my family was damaged.

Deanna Fredricks stood a mere 100 feet from us with a wicked grin on her face. A glowing, oval portal was just behind her swirling a liquid-like substance around in an arch that hummed and vibrated.

"Well, well. I finally get to meet the little brat who should have come from my body and not that tramp, Adelaide's. Too bad I couldn't pull off my diabolical plan before your old man left your mother and knocked me up instead. You'd be my little girl!"

"My father did not leave my mother. You spelled him, you..."

"You'd like to think that wouldn't you? Oh, no. Charlie Sweet came willingly into my bed, dearie. And don't you forget it. I gave him free will—his choice—whether or not to stay with me or return to try and find you and your Auntie Jess. He chose me. Charlie chose *me!*"

Pandora made a slight movement in my direction and touched her fingertips to my hand. I cut my eyes in her direction and she gave a barely imperceptible shake of her head. I didn't know what she was trying to tell me, however.

"He did not." Turning back to Deanna, I balled my hands into fists and fought the urge to go dark. I didn't know what I was dealing with and knew I had a difficult time controlling the siren magic, let alone the witch magic, and now I felt like a ticking time bomb with unknown power.

"Suit yourself. Believe your own reality. You will see. I know what you are trying to do. I know you think you can make a potion and call Charlie and expect him to fall for Adelaide again. It's been twenty-one years. Twenty-one years he's been warming my bed and giving me the children I so coveted. Oh! I'm sorry. Did that idea never once cross your mind? You have a bunch of half-siblings, Lily. They've all heard about their stupid dark witch older sister, and they all hate your guts."

I felt myself losing control and fought the urge to black out. The siren magic was in a battle for domination with my witch blood. Who knows what other blood was awakening and coiling up ready to explode in righteous fury?

"Easy, sugar."

Pandora side-whispered to me and took a step forward.

"Well, look what the swamp rat dragged in. How ya doin' skank?"

Deanna stared at Pandora for a long minute then her lip curled in derision.

"Do I know you?"

"You should."

"I don't think so. I don't bother with lesser beings, and you look like you dropped out of witch reform school."

As far as a comeback, it was pretty lame. I guessed Deanna never beheld Dorie outside her book form, so when she didn't comprehend who she was, it made sense.

"So, what, now. We fight? Two against one?" Pandora taunted the crazy loon.

"Oh, the time will come—very soon as a matter of fact. But I need to torture you a bit first...and warn you. Lily do not make that potion. Don't try and call Charlie to you. You will regret it."

"I think you are full of it, lady. You're even crazier than Donna...and she's certifiable," I said then crossed my arms over my chest.

"We shall see about that, why don't we? Oh, here...wait, someone would like to say something to you."

Waving her hand at the magic portal, a figure began to emerge, and I knew at once I'd be facing my father.

The man looked like a shell of his old self—or the photos I had of him and scrutinized for hours since being back in Sweet Briar. He was gaunt, unkempt, and had crazed eyes that darted this way and that as if waiting for some unknown entity to attack.

"Look who is here to meet you, Charlie! It's your first-born. This is Lily Sweet...your daughter. Adelaide's child."

The fury with which my father's face morphed made me sick in the pit of my stomach and I wanted to cry out in frustration.

"What does it want? Why bother me? I don't want any brat of Adelaide's. I hate that witch! This is no daughter of mine." He took a step in my direction and began waving his hands at me violently. "Go on. Get out of here. Leave me alone. You aren't my child. Let me be!"

I turned away and ran back up the path as fast as my legs would take me, the taunting laugh of Deanna Fredricks following behind. It wasn't that I couldn't handle the vitriol coming from my father. It wasn't that I was afraid of Deanna and had to scamper away like a rabbit running from the fox.

No.

I was so angry I was afraid I'd kill them both, Deanna

and Charlie, and leave them in a pile of blackened ash. I knew I had to find out if this was some kind of trickery before I let loose my magic, so my only option was retreat. *For now.*

I made it halfway back up the trail when out of nowhere a figure I least expected to see appeared out of thin air. My Great Aunt Moira was in front of me blocking the path to my Jeep.

"Ach, Lily. Stop a minute, lass. You need tae go back there. There's something for ye to see! I dinnae ken why that horrible woman appeared, but she tainted the wee loch and ye need to go turn it back. Ye need to free Tarni if she's trapped on the bottom. I've been watching the water. It glows deeply at night! So back!"

I stopped and looked over my shoulder, only now realizing Pandora had not followed me. Oh, great. Turning back to Aunt Moira to ask a question, I found her gone.

This was getting weirder and weirder.

Running back the way I'd come, I came to a stop when I saw Pandora lying flat on the ground with her face near the water. Oh, my gosh! Did Deanna harm her? Was she dead?

"Dorie!"

"Oh, my word will you stop screeching! I'm trying to concentrate!"

OK, then. Not dead.

"What are you doing down there?"

"Well, if you hadn't of hightailed it out of here at the first sign something isn't' quite right with Daddio, you'd have realized it was an illusion. Just as this pond is an illusion to discourage you from getting to Tarni."

"No. I just ran into the ghost of my Aunt Moira. She said the pond needs to be turned back to normal and we need to free Tarni if she is trapped below the surface. This is no illusion, it's..."

Pandora stood up and wiped her fingertips that she'd been swirling around in a clockwise motion on the surface of the pond. Within seconds, the water began to clear and before I knew it, Nichols Pond was the same incredible body of water it had been before today.

"OK...it was an illusion."

"Told ya," Pandora smiled.

But if this was an illusion, why hadn't Tarni come when I called? Maybe Deanna had injured her—or worse. Just as I was about to voice this fear, the surface of the pond began to bubble, and a light came shooting from its depths.

Instead of Tarni Vanderzee rising out of the water, a tiny glass bottle popped to the surface, and I would hear a song in my head calling to me to retrieve it. It was Tarni's voice. I couldn't make out any words but knew without a doubt that the glass vial held some of Tarni's tears. We did it. We had all we needed to call my father home!

Time to get back to Rudy and Adriana and inform them of all that transpired...and get that potion a-brewin'!

CHAPTER 18

When I walked into my home, the unusual continued when I found someone sitting at my kitchen table that I least expected to see.

"Jerry Godfather!"

"The one and only!" My Jerry Godfather jumped up and gave me an enthusiastic hug before turning to ogle Pandora. "And who do we have here? Wow, honey, with legs like those, you are going to wind up walking the catwalk for Victoria's Secret. Dang!"

Pandora would be more flattered if Jerry hadn't been wearing an evening gown, had a tiara on his head while sporting his trademark Louboutin's shoes—and in full makeup to boot. I just wish he'd shave that beard. I mean if you are going to be a cross-dressing fairy godfather—lose the hair already!

"It's so nice to see you on the surface! But who is guarding the Forbidden Library?"

"Oh, the Council got me an intern. Waste of good money. But at least it gives me a chance to come up and breathe the fresh air and see the sights."

Jerry cut his eyes to my Uncle Rudy, who was beaming even if he looked a bit flustered. Oh lord, please tell me a romance wasn't brewing between the two. I mean, Rudy was a Greek god, all chiseled perfection and model perfection. Jerry? Jerry looked like Danny Devito on a bender. I loved my fairy godfather, but someone dropped the bomb when they were handing out looks. But hey! To each his own, right? Love is in the eye of the beholder and all that. However, the way they were eying each other, it might just be lust!

"Name's Pandora. Charmed." Dorie shook Jerry's hand, which he immediately grasped in his, turned her palm upward, and dropped a kiss on her wrist. Pandora giggled and slapped his hand away.

Oh, brother.

We took the time to explain to the two men and my great-grandmother what had happened. A darkness overcame Adriana the likes I'd never seen before and hoped never to see again.

"Lies. All of them! Charlie would never leave Adelaide for Deanna. He would never abandon you nor would he leave his best friend hanging. He loved Jessica as well! He loved the three of you so much. Deanna is spreading doubt, so you will give up. It's obvious!"

I hope.

"Well, now is the time to act. Tarni left her tears behind for us. I guess she figured I might need more." I smiled shamefully, knowing in the past how topsy-turvy my magic could be. "What's the plan?"

"Now we call Charlie and ruin Deanna's life!" Adriana proclaimed.

"Not so fast. Ye hafta stop her, Lily. Adriana is aboot to go off her heid and it's no guid!" Aunt Moira popped in with Edith on her heels. Edith, Adriana could see and waved her away like a gnat when Edith moved to stop her from grabbing the ingredients to make the potion. Moira sighed. I decided it was time to inform Granny another ghost was hanging around me. This would not end well.

❧

WHAT DO you mean Moira is here! If Moira were here, I would think she'd tell me, I would see and hear her!"

"Apparently not," I said and winced when Adriana lobbed her gaze in my direction.

Gah!

"Um, I'm sorry. But Aunt Moira has been here since...well, since that day I asked you who she was in the photograph."

"Liliana! Do you mean to tell me you've kept this from me all this time? What kind of great-granddaughter are you?"

"Tell her tae stop it. Adriana's pure grabbit the day! Grumpy she is! We've no time tae waste! Hand this to her. Only ye can do it, lass."

Holding her hand out to me, I saw that Moira was holding a fancy lace hanky. A pretty white linen with tiny purple flowers embroidered on the edge. I knew Moira was once ghost who could manipulate matter, but would I be able to take something from her ghostly realm and bring it into mine? Reaching out, I tentatively touched the fabric and was amazed when it went from a see-through bit of ephemera to a solid piece of material!

"Give it to Annie!"

Adriana watched me with wide eyes as I approached and handed over the handkerchief. The minute she touched it, Moira appeared to her. I could tell this because my great-grandmother reared back and gasped. "Moira! Oh, my!"

After a bit of catching up on their part, Moira went on to tell me she'd managed to find the rift in the veil that Deanna used to travel back and forth at will. Very powerful magic, dark and forbidden, was something the renegade witch used with abandon, never once worrying about the consequences. I'd recently learned that all magic came with a price, even the innocent stuff like lighting a candle or cloaking oneself to become invisible. We weren't talking about earth-shattering repercussions, but vile magic? It would eventually lead to horrific ramifications and worse...madness.

Deanna was flirting with disaster at this point and Moira had witnessed firsthand just how awful a situation she was in.

"There be no wee bairns. She lied tae ye. Edith knows. I brought her with me so she would ken the situation!" Moira looked to Edith to continue.

"Deanna is as mad as a loon! Her mind was warped when she lived here before all these deceptions. Her mother did a number on her head—both she and Donna," said Edith. "But what no one realizes is tragic in a way—not that I'm making any excuses for Deanna. But she got into trouble as a teen and found herself pregnant. She always wanted what belonged to someone else, and the boy that got her pregnant was to marry a wealthy witch from a coven in North Carolina. When she told him she was pregnant, he gave her some money to get rid of it. She didn't want to, but he forced her, laughed at her. He told Deanna he was just sewing his oats before he settled down with a proper lady."

Edith floated over to the fireplace and looked at the photos hanging on the wall. "Deanna confided in Charlie...the one boy she knew from the area who never treated her like a slutty lowlife. But Charlie was in the middle of the drama surrounding Adelaide and her flirty ways and he made a grave mistake. In his anger at Adelaide for teasing him by trying to make him jealous with other boys, Charlie fired out words to Deanna he never meant—in his right mind anyway. He told Deanna it would be better off getting rid of her baby. She was too young and too poor to raise a baby. He was out of his mind with worry that Adelaide might wind up the same way. His words were meant to punish his own inability to be someone enough—so his hurt pride thought at the time—for the girl he'd fallen deeply in love with. He would never have told Deanna to do such a thing otherwise."

I pondered this a minute but remained confused. "Wait a minute. I don't understand. It's not as if my dad got Deanna pregnant. Why the hate? Why the jealousy?"

"Because Deanna chose to listen to Charlie, and in her mind she made up a tale that perhaps by doing this, getting rid of her child, Charlie might want her instead of Adelaide. With that other boy's baby gone, she would be pure again for Charlie. Only, she didn't dare go to a cleric. She went to a clinic in Atlanta—only human doctors cannot perform an abortion on a witch. Deanna was destroyed inside and out. She would never have a child of her own ever again. That's why we know she's lying about your having siblings," Edith declared.

"I didn't believe her," said Pandora. "I mean, I could see right through her glamour, but I get it—no disparity to you, Lily. The stress of seeing your father had to be clouding your judgment." She gave me an apologetic smirk and shrugged. "If it wasn't for the electric static, I might have been fooled as well."

"Wait! What electric static?" I asked.

Dorie looked at me incredulously. "Staring at them was like watching an old TV—or video cassette. They had lines going up and down their bodies. Hadn't you noticed?"

I had not.

"Haud on. There's another thing tae be mindful of," said Moira ominously. "Deanna has used such awful magic, she no right in her heid. She's pure dafty now! Ye must use trickery! Otherwise, she'll be on tae ye! Tell them, Edith!"

Edith turned to me and smiled. "I snooped in Nora's notes. She didn't know what she was getting into when she was trying to steal that sweetbriar ring from Nichols Pond. But I remember her going over family lore and trying to figure out what Deanna and Donna had been up to once she heard the rumors, then got confirmation it was them who did all these things. I stood over her shoulder yesterday and read some of the notes she was scribbling. Some of it was nonsense, silly rhymes or something. Others looked like spells. Much of it was notes on connecting the dots between all the players in this insane game...especially how they are tied to Lily." Edith looked proud and I gave her a thumbs up. "Nora was always too smart for her own good but never used it to help anyone—well, when she wants to or is made to feel guilty she might, but honestly, she's worked so much of this out, it's criminal."

"What do you mean?" asked Adriana.

"I mean Nora knows how to win against Deanna and didn't bother sharing it with her own family. Instead, she told Wilhelmina and Boris—and my family told her to take it to her grave. Can you imagine? My family is horrid!"

I wasn't surprised. The Dietrichs and the Langsfords hated my great-grandmother even though we'd tried to mend fences. Well—maybe not so much on Adriana's part.

"How do we best her?" asked Adriana with interest.

"When Deanna teamed up with Lucretia, she begged to be turned into a vampire. So Lucretia acquiesced," Edith proclaimed to a stunned room.

"But she herself was turned and would not create a powerful vampire. Deanna might be mostly undead—so we stake her!" Adriana argued.

I sat down hard...on the ground. I didn't even check to see if there was a chair behind me. There wasn't. *Ow.* It hadn't occurred to me that I was "mostly undead" myself, now that I knew that I was a vampire!

"Liliana! Stop playing games. Get up." Adriana scolded me.

I guess she couldn't tell I was having a small panic attack on the floor. Maybe she was hard of hearing and mistook my whimpers for Wicked meowing. I have too many Breed in me! I fondly recalled the day I found out I was a witch and chuckled at my dismay upon learning I was a witch. The poor fool. What I wouldn't do to go back to that moment—then run shrieking for the hills and then escape back to New York State. I'd never know I was a creature of the night. Oh lord, I hope I don't have wings and can morph into a bat. I rolled over into the fetal position and contemplated checking into a mental hospital. Who would take me though?

"So let me get this straight," said Adriana looking askance at me as I began to moan. "Only a vampire can kill another vampire of a certain age. That is what Caliente stated when she told us about Gertrude and how her attack on the vampire lair was targeted toward the younglings. Younglings and young adult vampires anyone can kill. But the older ones...we can stake them, freeze them by the right tool. We can even put them in a firepit and have them perpetually roast—although it won't do them in. But to eradicate them completely, another vampire must do the task, right?"

"In a manner of speaking, yes," said Edith. "Another vampire can kill Deanna...but it has to be a vampire related by blood."

All eyes in the room turned toward me. I wasn't looking my best at the moment, seeing as I had begun to chant a little song about not worrying and being happy. It must have finally gotten through to everyone that I was Not. Doing. OK.

It wasn't that the news that I was the one who must take on Deanna freaked me out. It wasn't that I had to drink the potion and release the spell I concocted and call my father home. It wasn't even all the Breed blood I had coursing through my veins. It was the fact that I hadn't even been in the paranormal world a year yet, and suddenly the weight of it all was too much. I needed a hug. Or a cookie. Or to go back in time and smoke that joint I'd refused at my first college party—such a goody-goody. Although that might have been a good thing. Maybe smoking some pot would have let my vampire out and the common area would have turned into a blood bath.

Everyone expected me to go, "Huh, interesting!" and instantly get with the program. But they had all grown up knowing who and what they were. They had years of training, schooling, familial advice, and practice. They didn't grow up in a world where humans loved to watch scary movies, firm in their beliefs that it was all make-believe movie stuff. Let's face it...I *am* the something that goes bump in the night!

CHAPTER 19

At least I was given one more night of rest—not like I got any sleep for very long. I tossed and turned until Wicked, having enough, swatted my head, spit, and ran off to go sleep in Adelaide's room. I know I dropped off eventually, but the sun came up too soon and so did Adriana.

Yes. Up. I was startled awake when I sensed someone in my room and found her standing over me with a long dagger.

"Holy cannoli! What do you think you are doing old woman? Are you crazy?" I shrieked.

Pandora came waltzing into the room eating one of my wax apples. I stared at her, and she shrugged. "What? I found it on the floor and thought it was real."

"Yet you are still eating it?"

"I'm hungry!"

"Are you ever not hungry?"

"Only when I'm sated from too much wild..."

"OK, moving on. Why are you up here, both of you?

And what's with the dagger?" Turning to Adriana, I gave her my fiercest scowl. She just cackled then her face got somber again.

"I wanted to force you to punch your fangs out. It's D-Day and you can't even figure out how to do it. How are you going to win this fight?"

"D-Day?" I asked.

"Do Deanna In Day," replied Adriana who began looking through my chest of drawers with Dorie.

"That doesn't correlate. Wouldn't that make it D, D, Day? Or D, D I, Day?" I needed more sleep. "Hey! Get out of there. What are you doing?"

"Finding you an outfit to fight in," said Pandora, throwing me a wink.

"I do not need help picking out an outfit to wear. I am perfectly capable of dressing myself. I'm..."

"No, not that one. It makes her ass look fat." Adriana tossed a favorite pair of slacks onto the floor and opened another drawer.

"Adelaide gave me perfectly acceptable fighting clothing. I intend to wear that."

"No. You are not."

I blinked and regarded Adriana who was holding up a Motley Crüe tee and shaking her head. "They had like eight good songs. I mean really! Even "Dr. Feelgood" gets old after a while."

Pandora was nodding her head in agreement. "I much prefer Bon Jovi," she said.

Adriana snorted.

"What? They are the better band!"

"For lightweights."

"Bon Jovi are not lightweights! You take that back!" Pandora cried.

I was getting a headache.

"I bet you think Engelbert Humperdick..."

"Humperdinck!" I shouted.

"Whatever! I bet you think they are the best rock band around."

"No, I don't," said Adriana.

"You do too!"

"No, I don't because he's a man, not a band. Get yourself a better appreciation for music, dear."

And this was how my morning started. It could only get better from here, right?

Humperdinck!

"What do you mean my mother will be bait?"

It got worse. Very worse.

I'd gotten myself dressed—alone. And yes, I chose my own outfit. Then I went downstairs to find everyone I knew eating breakfast in my kitchen, den, and sunporch. I'm not even going to go over the list. Everyone was present and accounted for that had a vested interest in the outcome of today.

Brian was the last to arrive and he looked haggard and like a week's worth of sleep wouldn't be enough to make up for the long days and nights he'd put in searching for those missing. Ah, yes. The feed from the school gave us the make and model of the mystery man, Alan's, vehicle. It was a white van. Go figure.

And the police found him, in all places, at Doreen and Donald Murphy's motel. My dear friends had no idea he was wanted for questioning. He appeared to them to be a mild-mannered, average guy who was looking to sell his birdhouses at the fairgrounds. Nothing out of the ordinary, that is, until Sheriff Glen Buford and Brian went to check out the stand-alone building the Murphys rented out for larger parties and found all of our missing residents bound, drugged, and most importantly—unharmed!

Deanna paid Alan to kidnap the townsfolk who had a connection to me but were easy targets. Alan used a blow dart provided by Deanna to stun our friends and neighbors, making them pliable and obedient. Then all he had to do was lead them to his van and drive them to the motel. The cottage he was in was tucked away from the main building and it was easy enough to conceal his actions from the Murphys. It rubbed me wrong when I found out the man wasn't even paranormal. Alan was a human who had no idea how bad a situation he had gotten himself into. Glen Buford dragged him kicking and screaming in protest to the jail. He insisted he believed it was an elaborate prank and no harm would have come to our friends.

It truly was a total distraction ploy and one that had its merits—we were certainly distracted enough to bring in hellhounds.

Speaking of hellhounds, Max and Rex were to be my bodyguards today. When I called my dad with the spell, the dogs would flank my side in anticipation of Deanna dropping in to ruin the reunion. We hoped they would give Deanna pause and allow me to do my thing. What that thing *is* was yet to be determined.

"My mother is not going to be bait. Wait. Bait for what? How?"

"Well, it makes sense to put her out in the open so the magic you release that calls our Charlie brings him to an area where we can all be hidden and jump out to aid you if Deanna brings an army of crazed Romanos and other renegades, no?" Lizzie stated.

OK, I hated to admit it, but it did make sense.

"Where then? My yard?" I asked.

"I'd hate to have the lot of us trample your garden, but I can't think of a better spot," said Lou. "Wait a minute! How about we settle her directly in the back near the Reids gate? They have wonderful mature shrubs and magnolias we can hide under and around...and this way, you'd have your house behind you, your Jeep on one side and on the far side, we can park another SUV with a few of us tucked down in there as well."

"Yeah, and those two big brutes can flank you on either side. It could work." Uncle Rudy was tending to the potion still swirling away in the cauldron. We hadn't added the siren tear to the elixir because we wanted it to be as potent as possible.

Max and Rex were snoring on my side porch, drool was pooling on the floorboards such that it looked like I'd placed birdbaths under their heads!

I set up a little table beside them and that was where Rudy sat watching over the contents of the cauldron.

"What do we suspect will happen? What about surprises? What might Deanna have up her sleeve that we hadn't counted on?" I asked this question in light of all the recent events where the unexpected became the norm. It might be a good thing—for me, anyway—to hear some possibilities bantered about.

Andrea was sitting on the porch step next to me and we were both watching Lorcan as he watered the sweetbriar rose.

Adriana was sitting on a lawn chair beside Antonio, who still had a difficult time meeting everyone's eyes. Impulsively, I stood and ran to him, throwing my arms around him in a big hug. "I'm glad you're here, Gramps! Maybe we can work on my fangs while the others figure out strategy."

Antonio gazed up at me with tears in his eyes. "Liliana, mi dispiace..."

"Don't you dare apologize to me! Who knows? I might make a stellar vamp! Fangs could become my fashion statement. And hey! I won't need a costume for Halloween!"

He reached up and patted the hand I had resting on his shoulder, but I could see it would take some time for him to accept I didn't lay the blame on him or Pandora for what happened to me as a child.

Speaking of Pandora, she'd spent the morning reading the *Book of Loves Lost* that Jerry brought with him. Jerry was going over it and the two of them were arguing the benefits of using one spell over another. I had no interest in debating with them over something I was uncertain about, so I let them have at it.

"What about a trap? Perhaps Deanna has something planned that will give us false hope then she springs something else that will take us out in a blaze of glory," suggested Andrea.

"Not Bon Jovi again. Give it up already!" Adriana barked, causing Dorie to shoot her a dark look.

Adriana blew a raspberry her way.

It suddenly occurred to me that everyone was keeping things light for my benefit, but I could see the underlying worry and it was making me anxious. Just the fact that Adriana woke me up by hovering over me with my mother's—no, *my*—dagger, had me seeing the seriousness of my situation. I'd have to be a fool not to see it. I think they knew the unexpected was coming, and I wasn't quite prepared to the extent I needed to be in light of the fact I needed fangs.

Here's the thing. Even if I managed to make the buggers descend, would I be able to bring myself to sink them into Deanna's neck at the opportune time and bite her to death or…?

"Hey. I just thought of something. No one has explained how I am to kill Deanna. Do I bite her? Impale her? If I don't need to bite her—why do I need my fangs to descend? Wouldn't the element of surprise be better if she thought I was just a witch or a blend of witch and shifter…and even siren? Deanna has no idea about what happened to Antonio and me."

Do you know what it's like to have an entire group of people stare at you in stupefaction and contemplate your words, only to see understanding dawn? And what was once cloaked uneasiness in your abilities turn into admiration and relief?

Yeah…*that* happened.

"Oh, Lily. You're brilliant!" Becky Nolan, Jake's girlfriend, and my good friend, enthused.

"We were so focused on the newness of finding out what Lily is, it made us get bogged down in the details!" Jerry cried.

"That's it!" squealed Pandora. "That's how Lily is going to win today. That's how she will have and keep a leg up on this loser. Lily needs to be prepared for the unexpected and wait for Deanna to show her hand. Obviously, she will use the element of surprise and extend her fangs. Instead of Lily informing the enemy that she too, is a vampire, she needs to act defeated. Let Deanna get close in —I assume the fangster will try and take a nibble out of our darling girl, and when she is in just the right spot? Bam! Lily strikes."

"How? What does Lily need to do?" Aunt Chiara asked.

"Oh, well…it's simple really," said Abner. He popped up out of nowhere as usual, but since he was holding a hoe, I assumed he'd been gardening. "Lily just has to impale her, rendering her harmless..."

Hmm...that isn't so bad. I could do that!

"...and once Deanna is down for the count, Lily needs to drain her of all her blood!"

Oh, crud.

CHAPTER 20

The men made a makeshift bed and carried Adelaide down, placing her gently on top where she resembled every fairytale princess awaiting a kiss from her prince. Everyone else was setting up hiding spots that would conceal them from any and all backup Deanna brought with her. A surprise attack from our side would hopefully even the playing field.

I was dressed in my best fighting outfit that Adelaide had made for me, and I tucked the special hawthorn stake in a secret pocket near my left wrist. I had two backup ones made of willow on either hip. I reached up in a vain attempt to loosen the many braids my long hair has been woven into. Better to have it back and out of the way instead of getting in my face—or getting pulled. I was itching to use the siren tear in my potion, but Pandora, Jerry, and now Uncle Rudy, were still fighting over which of the many passages to use.

"That doesn't even rhyme!" complained Pandora, grabbing one of those small pencils you use to fill out lottery tickets and circling the verse in question.

"Woman, you are trying my patience! How can you not see true can be paired with groove? It doesn't have to be perfect to work! It's all in the delivery. Lily just needs to add a bit of pizzazz to her recitation!" Jerry pulled out his high-end marker and X'd out the circle Dorie drew.

"You're daft!" Pandora tossed the pencil in the air and knocked the Jerry marker on the ground. I grabbed the pencil before it could bop me in the face, and went to tuck it behind my ear, but missed and felt it enter one of my braids. Great. It would take weeks for me to untangle the mess and retrieve the darn thing!

I leaned down and got in Pandora's face.

"Listen, Dorie. One, you almost poked my eye out. Watch what you are throwing. Two, it doesn't have to be a perfect verse, just something that makes the most sense in this situation. We need to order my dad to ignore everything else in his world and come find his true love. I mean, how hard can this be? And three...well, I don't have a three. Let's just pick a spell and get this over with! And if you two don't stop squabbling, I am going to give you crayons and you can start coloring the pictures in that book!"

"Why don't you use this one?" Jake wandered over and picked up a piece of paper with a delicate handwritten poem on it.

"Where did you get that?"

"It fluttered out of the book just now...I think. Anyway, look at the words. They fit this situation perfectly!" Jake shoved the note under my nose and I grabbed it, smoothed it out, and placed it on the table so we could all read it together:

Lover mine return to me

Whether by land or sea
Ignore the ties that bind your heart
Return to the one who captured your heart
When you arrive by siren tear
She will be there, and you will be here
But not before it pricks your heart
Catch the doll our life will start
Lover mine return to me
Listen to my plea

"THAT'S KIND OF DISJOINTED. It's not a very good poem. Although *some* words do apply to our situation," Jerry offered. "I don't know. A few of the lines need reworking because they are nonsensical."

"I like how it says she will be there, and you will be here. Maybe it's a way of bringing Charlie to us and leaving Deanna behind. A win-win!" Jake declared.

"I don't know. It's a lousy cadence...it's all wrong!" Pandora was fretting again but something about the verse hit me in the pit of my stomach. It was almost calling to me. How odd.

"I want to use it."

"Are you sure, sugar? I'm sure we could find something better," suggested Pandora.

"No. This is the one. I want to use it."

I handed the paper to Rudy and set the bottle containing the siren tears next to it. Turning to Pandora, I had one more question for her before I tried out the spell.

"Dorie. When you made it across the nation and landed in Deanna's camp, how many followers did she have with her?"

Pandora thought a moment, scratching her head in

concentration. "You know? She had so many wandering stragglers around, if I had to do an actual headcount, I couldn't come up with an accurate number. I mean, right around where Deanna stood with Charlie? Possibly ten coven members? But I could hear several sounds coming from nearby that gave me the impression she had a small army making war preparations. The sounds were unmistakable. So, who knows? But I'm worried we'll definitely be outnumbered. But can they fight? Are they as strong as us with their magic? That's the real question."

"Everything is ready then. Adriana decided. Liliana, add the tear and drink a tablespoon of the elixir. Then recite the verse. We must be prepared for the unexpected and the unknown. Remember...we don't know how our Charles will be. He might even attack Adelaide Above all else, protect Adelaide and then Lily."

I uncorked the bottle and added one drop—just one—of Tarni's precious tears, noticing there were quite a few left in the bottle. I hoped that meant she willed them to me to use for future projects and not a hint of what she thought my chances were crafting this spell.

I watched as the liquid in the cauldron went from amber to black and then an exact shade of purple like the ones I had painted in my hair. I took this as a good omen.

Just as I reached for a tablespoon, I felt a tickle of fur on my ankles. Looking down, I spied Wicked looking up at me. "What is it, Wicked? I will be just fine. Please don't chase the hellhounds away—I kind of need them for backup."

"Mroo?" Wicked jumped onto the table and that's when I noticed something dangling in her mouth. It was the tiny yin-yang charm that Charlie had made for me when I was a baby. I placed it on a silver chain but hardly wore it now, my sweetbriar rose jewelry remained on me at all times. But seeing as my intelligent furball brought it out to me especially, I slipped it on. Hey, it couldn't hurt, right? I fumbled blindly until I felt warm hands brush against my neck and knew Lorcan was helping me.

Once around my neck, Wicked gave a tiny sneeze of approval, then zoomed around the house like a maniac. At least she went in the opposite direction from the hellhounds.

I turned to find Lorcan smiling at me then he leaned in and kissed my forehead. "Knock 'em dead, Tink. Be careful, OK?"

"I love you, Lor."

"I love you too, Lily."

I noticed my Uncle Rudy waving to get my attention.

"Lily. Don't forget my blood will counter the last spell," he said. "This time there won't be a koosh ball flying through the air trying to find Charlie's one true love. This time it will be Charlie flying to us by magic. He shouldn't be able to fight the magic and will appear rather quickly—or so we hope. The potion we crafted is supercharged to work immediately."

Lorcan stepped back, and I looked down at the items on the table.

Stirring the mixture, I dipped the tablespoon in and gave it one more gentle stir, then I scooped up a level measurement and put the spoon in my mouth.

Blech!

I locked eyes with my Uncle Rudy who made a sympathetic face and motioned I should swallow. But I couldn't! Turning in alarm to glance at Lorcan I could see he was worried but didn't know how to help me. No matter how easy one would think swallowing liquid should be, no matter how many times I made the attempt, I couldn't manage to have what tasted like old socks slide down my throat.

I thought all hope was lost until I heard Adriana come up behind me and before I could turn around to see what she would do, I felt her smack the back of my head.

Gulp!

"All better? Good. Recite!"

I was going to brain that old woman someday. I swear it.

I picked up the piece of paper and went to stand between Max and Rex who greeted me with soft "woofs" and plenty of drool. Their tail thumping alone was causing the weeds in my backyard to bend in the breeze. I waited until those who had been with me on the porch had taken their set hiding positions and opened my mouth.

But that's the exact moment Wicked came running back to me. This time she had the poppet in her mouth and dropped it at my feet.

"Wicked! I don't have time for games! Go put this back...hey!" That darn cat ran back the way she'd come, completely ignoring the cowering hounds. Great. I needed these two in battle mode and they just peed in fear of a critter the size of their one paw! Not a good omen!

Sighing, I picked up the poppet and tucked it into my back pocket, then I checked one last time that I could reach the hawthorn stake with lightning speed. That confirmed, I made eye contact with Adriana who was directly in front of me, just behind Eileen Reid's prized rhododendron, and I began to speak the words on the paper.

I said the words loud and clear, tracking my eyes to Pandora who stood to the left of Adriana, Aunt Moira and Edith just behind, nodding their encouragement. Just as I reached the last line, I allowed my eyes one brief glance in my mother's direction. Lorcan remained hidden in the bush just beyond her makeshift bed. Our eyes connected.

As I uttered the last word, two things occurred that altered my perception of what was going to happen next. One, Adelaide opened her eyes and sat up, turning to me with a smile. And two, Nora stepped out from behind the rock wall on the edge of my yard and gave me a self-satisfied look.

Then everything around me shifted and I felt myself flying through a wind tunnel.

CHAPTER 21

I felt myself spiraling down in an almost vortex-like circling pattern minus the water. Yet I wasn't in any kind of atmosphere. It almost felt like I was swimming in a river of foam. Then I wasn't moving any longer yet remained, shockingly, on two feet.

I had my eyes squeezed shut, but hurriedly opened them lest I be caught at a disadvantage. I'm glad I did. Standing not twenty paces from me was Deanna Fredricks leaning over the prostrate form of my father, Charlie.

"What did you do to him?" she shrieked.

Whoa. The sheer magnitude of her hatred and insanity hit me like a bolt of lightning and I felt dizzy with the taint of her magic that swirled and coiled in the very air around us.

"How did you get here? What are you doing?"

How did I get here? I assumed this was the trickery we worried about, and instead of Charlie going to Adelaide's side, somehow Deanna cast a counter spell that had me going to where they were camped.

"Where are we?" I asked instead.

"How should I know. One minute I was in my compound and suddenly I'm here in this...this...wherever this is. How did you manage this trickery?"

"Is it just the two of you, no one else is with you?" Again, I responded to Deanna's queries with a question of my own.

"Look at him! I think you killed my Charlie. Look what you've done!"

I felt the icy-hot essence of my magic kick on, recognizing at once that my witch magic was competing with my siren magic. I took in a deep breath via my diaphragm, then let it out slowly through my mouth. I remained focused and willed the two parts of me to work together. Within seconds, I could feel the shift as the magic entwined and began to work together and coil up and out of me.

"He isn't your Charlie. He never was and he never will be," I said in a soft voice.

"Don't you dare say those words to me. Twenty-one years Charlie has been mine. He will never go back to your precious Adelaide. Never!" Deanna was practically frothing at the mouth, her eyes wild and her energy foul.

"Adelaide."

We both looked down to where my father now lay blinking and unfocused.

"Adelaide," he repeated her name, almost reverently.

"No! I forbid this. What dark magic are you doing? I forbid you to ruin all my plans!" Deanna flashed so quickly I had no time to react and felt the searing pain as her dagger-sharp nails raked my face, narrowly missing my eyes.

"You bitch! Leave us alone! I should have killed you when you were a baby. I should have taken what I wanted and left you both for dead. Instead, I listened to my idiot sister, Donna. I showed mercy. Look what it got me. You are here trying to take my heart's desire from me!"

"Charlie Sweet would never be yours. You stupid woman. If you have to keep him by your side with magic, he was never yours to begin with. Even now the spell I concocted is working. The spell was a success. Look at him. He hears my mother calling."

Indeed, with every passing second, Charlie Sweet lost some of the fogginess, which was replaced with confusion, but also something else...hope. Then his eyes landed on Deanna and his face darkened. "Where is Adelaide? Where is she?"

"No! Stop it, stop it, stop it. Now! This instant. Charlie, darling...we belong together. You are mine."

"I'm not yours. My heart belongs to Adelaide." Turning in my direction, a look of wonder and recognition crossed Charlie Sweet's face. "Do I know you? I feel like I do."

Before I could reply, Deanna flashed once more and lifted me up easily then tossed me toward my father where I landed in a heap of hurt and anger. OK, she might be a middling vampire, but she was still plenty strong. I felt a bone pop somewhere, but I couldn't feel any pain. This wasn't good.

I was going to kill this woman if it was the last thing I did. I stood up on shaky legs and growled.

Just as I moved to defend myself, I saw my father look down on the ground at the poppet doll that must have fallen out of my pocket. He reached out and picked it up.

Then he disappeared.

"No! What did you do? Where did he go?" Deanna howled in incredulity and charged at me. Slamming into me at breakneck speed this time, we both wound up on the ground, Deanna above me, teeth bared, thenshe began to slam my head up and down.

I punched the side of her head then went for her eyes.

Howling, she rolled off me and retreated across the playing field. That was the only way to describe where we wound up. Some kind of otherworldly arena, glowing dark green around the edges with no discernable top, bottom, or sides. I knew I was on a flat surface, but I couldn't begin to describe it. It felt like we were suspended in a green cube above an alien world.

Or not. My head ached.

"I'm sorry about the baby, you know. I hate that you faced such a choice at such a young age. And I think it's horrible what happened. But none of that was my fault—or my family's!"

"Don't you dare offer me your pity. I don't want it. I don't need it. You worthless cur!"

So much for trying to be nice.

We were circling each other now, Deanna's eyes roaming all over me as if sizing up her competition and finding it lacking.

"You can quit pretending it wasn't you who brought me here. How did you do it? Where are we anyway? Too bad it only half worked. That doll took my dad right to Adelaide's side. I'm certain of this. I bet they are wrapped around each other even as we waste time fighting like this. It's over Deanna...you lose."

Screaming, the vampire witch launched at me, but this time I was prepared. I did a fancy sidestep my mother taught me and watched as Deanna went flying by, arms waving like windmills as she tried to regain her balance. When she came to a halt, she turned in a flash. And that's when I noticed her fangs were out.

I remembered what I was counseled to do and

pretended shock and fear followed by the look of defeat. Deanna's eyes lit up and she became triumphant in her demeanor. Throwing her shoulders back and tossing her tangled mass of hair from her face, her words came out fast, and this time I could easily tell, riddled with lies.

"Poor Lily. You've lost. Even now, my people are raiding your village and slaughtering everyone in their path. So what? Adelaide has Charlie. For now, my dear. Only for the briefest moment. When I am done with you, I will call my champion and she will lead me directly to my Charlie's side. Then I will personally kill your mother and have everything I've ever wanted in an instant. I just may move into your little house with Charlie. Wouldn't that be wonderful?"

I reached down to my wrist, feeling for the stake but coming up empty.

Uh, oh.

"Looking for this, dearie?"

In Deanna's hand was not only the hawthorn stake, but both willow ones I'd hidden for backup. This was not good.

"You know what? I think you are a nervous wreck and I just realized you were telling the truth about one thing. You didn't bring me here. Someone else had a hand in the spell crafting and that's how we both wound up in this place." My mind recalled the look on Nora's face at the last minute and I was almost certain it was her scribbled note we chose to read aloud to bring my dad home. Edith was right, Nora *was* working on a magic spell the night Edith peeked over her shoulder.

"It's of no consequence. Your family and friends can't help you here. But my champion can always find me. Ah! Here she is now." I watched Deanna react to a presence behind me and made myself turn to see who had appeared. My heart plummeted to my stomach when I saw Pandora standing behind me with dead eyes.

"END her now and I will bring you to Charlie's side," Pandora said in a voice I'd never heard come from her in all the time I'd known her. It was devoid of feeling and sent chills coursing through me.

"Dorie? Please tell me this isn't true. Please tell me this is some kind of joke."

"I'm tired of this, Deanna. End this creature's life. Now."

Before I could react, Pandora grabbed me by the throat and tossed me the short distance toward Deanna. I hit the ground hard and felt something else snap.

Deanna reached down and grabbed the top of my head, the pain from being lifted by my braids had me second-guessing my decision to tie my hair back. Jeebers that hurt!

I could feel Deanna running the hawthorn stake along my skin and knew I'd probably lost the battle. At least I knew my parents were together and my family would fight to the death to protect them. I just wished there was a way for me to warn them about Pandora. She must have been working with Nora. No... that couldn't be right. Deanna was shocked that we'd been brought to this place. And it gave my dad time to grab the poppet. As much as I hated to admit it, Nora had helped.

It didn't matter now.

Oh, I wasn't giving up. I'm a dark witch after all. And I would fight to the death with my head held high—for the most part.

I felt Deanna drag me over to a gnarled and knobby tree-like formation and she slammed my back hard into its rough surface. Lifting my arms above my head, she held me in place then moved her face inches from mine. Deanna smiled an evil smile and leaned over to graze her teeth along my neck. The pain was excruciating, and I felt my legs buckle. That's when Pandora came up on the other side of me just as I was about to use the last of my energy and release my magic. Instead, I felt a burst of pain as Pandora drove a willow stake into my side.

"I'm tired of playing with food. Let's end her and get out of here."

I can't believe I trusted the demon and felt a curse form on my lips. I could no longer move.

"This has been decades in the making and I want to torture this creature. The joy is in the victory and the knowledge. I have all the time in the world to make her suffer. Charlie isn't going anywhere. Anyway...I know where to find him now, don't I?" Deanna chuckled then gave me a side look. "I think after I tire of playing with this pathetic cur, I'll be ready for a snack. Perhaps I will dine on a certain black cat tonight. You did bring her with you, no?"

I watched in horror as a bored-looking Pandora lifted a lifeless-looking Wicked up in one hand. My poor girl was dangling and looked already dead. Before I knew what was happening, my fangs descended.

"What trickery is this? This cannot be! Neither of the families has vampire blood! Explain this to me at once!" Deanna fell back a few steps releasing my wrists which remained above my head.

That's when Pandora dropped a now-aware Wicked to the ground at the same time she pulled the stake out of me.

"Hey, sugar. I broke that lousy twig. How about you use that pencil sticking out of your head and we go have us some fun?"

Dorie!

I didn't waste a second in wonderment but launched myself in Deanna's direction, pulling the ridiculously mundane lottery pencil out of my braid. I jammed it as hard as I could into Deanna's neck.

Then I followed with a bite.

I could feel the life ebbing and flowing from Deanna Fredricks and sat back, straddling her as she became a stiff and useless board under me. Only her eyes could move, and they pleaded even as the hate remained. Wicked came over and jumped onto Deanna's chest and she looked deeply into those eyes. I could see the realization come over Deanna—the irony that the very cat she's imprisoned her enemy in for twenty-one years was now sitting atop her dying body smiling down as the life flowed out of her.

Wicked sneezed then jumped away and trotted over to Pandora.

"You had me fooled a moment you know."

"Yeah. But I knew those pearly points would eventually pop out if I did."

The surrealness of having this conversation while a woman lay dying under me didn't go unnoticed by me. But I couldn't bring myself an ounce of sympathy for this person who would most assuredly take pleasure in the slaughter of everyone I held dear.

It kind of put things in perspective.

"That stupid pencil. Can you believe it? Every time I play the lottery from now on I'm going to break out in a fit of the giggles."

"Lily. You're crying, honey. Get up off of her and come sit by me a sec, OK?"

I wasn't only crying. I was shaking and felt sick to my stomach.

I wobbled over to Pandora and we both sat down and

dangled our feet over the edge of a cliff, or whatever it was we were sitting on.

"Where are we anyway?"

"Oh, somewhere beyond," she replied.

"Beyond where?" I asked.

Sighing, Dorie turned and brushed a smudge of something off my face. "Beyond Earth."

OK, then.

Wicked trotted over and jumped in my lap where she curled up into a tiny perfect ball and began to purr.

"I'm going to be sore tomorrow, aren't I?"

"Like a mother," Pandora chuckled. "But I might be convinced to heal you before you feel anything too severe."

"Oh? And what would I owe you if you did that for me?"

"A trip to Paris and all the food I can stuff in my face while we're there."

I could live with that.

"Deal."

"Um, Lily? It's over."

Glancing at Deanna, I could see her glazed eyes and knew Dorie was speaking the truth.

"I don't feel anything, Dorie. Does that mean I'm...am I..."

"You want to know if you've become a heartless, evil demon filled with hatred and lusting for power now. Right?" Pandora tilted her head forcing me to look her in the face.

"Maybe?"

"Oh, sugar. You have nothing to worry about. There isn't an evil bone in your body. You didn't pick this battle. But you did choose to end it and save your dad. He's waiting for you, you know. Come on, stand up. We have a reunion to attend."

"I'm covered in blood and gore and that's how I'm attending the party. Yay me."

"Get used to it, kid. I have a feeling your troubles are just starting. Once word gets out you are the new big bad dark witch vampire hybrid thingy, you are going to draw all kinds of crazies to challenge you. It will be a hoot!"

I clutched Wicked to my chest and felt the exhaustion weighing me down even as I felt a shift in the air pressure all around me. I knew Pandora was doing her thing and I'd be standing in my backyard shortly surrounded by everyone I loved beyond reason.

My world was about to change one more time.

Slipping into my world again, I was hit with the sounds and smells familiar yet alien at the same time. I felt a throbbing in my temple and could smell the blood of all those who rushed at me.

Wicked jumped from my arms and scampered off to places unknown and I could make out the many voices of my loved ones, yet I was having a difficult time understanding anyone. The voices came at me twofold. I heard words as everyone shouted things at me, but at the same time, I could hear their thoughts and knew the vampire in me was strong.

I was trying to speak, but I couldn't find the words and wished above all else the noise would cease.

The buzzing of bees and birdsong became a symphony. I could hear conversations a mile away taking place in Joe's Diner. The sun's rays scorched and burned but not in a way that I felt threatened. I could even hear my own heartbeat and sense the movement of blood as it rushed through my body, and I suspected this would be something alien to a full-blooded vampire who didn't have blood of their own any longer.

Boy, was this going to be some learning curve.

I almost wished I was drunk on wine and dancing to an imaginary orchestra playing Vivaldi again.

I slowly felt the routine coming back as my hearing returned to normal. Then everything in my world tilted once more as I became aware of a figure approaching in my line of vision until his form was the only thing that filled the space in front of me.

Looking up into a face so familiar yet so very foreign, I absorbed the energy and love he was emitting even before his words registered. Our eyes locked and I heard the voice I'd been longing to hear my entire life say, "Hello, Lily. I'm Charlie. I'm your father."

THANK YOU FOR READING! I hope you loved meeting Lily and Lorcan, and the rest of the characters. The next book in the Lily Sweet Mysteries is I Spell Trouble. Find out if Charlie Sweet will be able to come to terms with his new reality or will depression and darkness threaten his very soul? And can Lily help her dad, or will her own troubles being a hybrid of so many Breed keep her from enjoying the victory over her enemies and run her chances at happiness...and love?

CLICK HERE TO READ I SPELL TROUBLE NOW>

And if you enjoyed Witch Way Did He Go?, you'll love Maggie and her quirky, sometimes funny, sometimes dark, but always magical paranormal gang of monster-hunting antique appraisers. A Tale of Two Sisters, the tie-in series to my Lily Sweet World, highlights Lily's cousins Maggie and Ellie Fortune and is FREE on Kindle Unlimited!

"I am loving the snark in this book."

- S. Keller, BookBub author reviews.

I appreciate your help in spreading the word, including telling friends and family. Reviews help readers find books! Please leave a review on your favorite book site.

You can also join my Facebook Group: Author Bettina M. Johnson's Team Wicked for exclusive giveaways and sneak peek of future books—and just plain silliness!

SIGN UP FOR BETTINA M. JOHNSON'S NEWSLETTER: http://eepurl.com/gZKo51

Continue on for a short excerpt from I Spell Trouble...

I Spell Trouble

"Coffee? Check. Pastries? Check. Fresh flowers? Che...hey! Wicked! Stop chewing on that arrangement, you demented furball. Get off the table!"

The last thing I needed today was a surly cat causing trouble and even one speck of anything out of place. Today was a very special day. Today both of my parents were coming home!

The old adage—*be careful what you wish for*—was running through my head as I looked out my kitchen window for the hundredth time this morning. You see, I am awaiting the return of my father, Charlie, and mom, Adelaide, from a hospital-like retreat they'd been away at for the last two weeks to try and have the witch clerics figure out what tracings of dark magic might still be swirling around inside my dad.

Our meeting had been bittersweet. I'd vanquished the evil Deanna Fredricks and the act of picking up the poppet had transported Charlie to my backyard and waiting family and friends, the most important of all being Adelaide—his long, lost love.

I missed witnessing their reunion because, yeah—battling an evil asshat of a witch!

My cousin Andrea said my two parents seeing each other for the first time in twenty-one years was the stuff of fairytales. But they didn't quite get their happily ever after as of yet. My father instantly began having dark magic withdrawals and despite him greeting me when I crossed back to where everyone was waiting for me to return, he'd become weakened and nauseous—so the paramedics were called.

My last image of the man had been his wild-eyed look and he was strapped to the gurney and a withered hand reaching for my mom. They had called from the hospital that he was being transferred to a witch's retreat, part spa part mental hospital where the foulest of magic could safely be expunged at the hands of some highly talented physicians in our magical world.

So, two long weeks of waiting had gone by, and now Charlie Sweet was finally coming home.

Those weeks would have been intolerable had my cousin's Maggie and Ellie Fortune not come down from North Carolina with their antique caravan. Although, with a murder happening and a psychotic stalker to deal with who decided Maggie would be his at all costs, things hadn't been as relaxing and fun as we'd hoped. At least it got my mind off my parents!

I promised my cousins that I'd head up to Mystic Valley, where they lived, when they were back at their family compound and not traveling all over the US selling and appraising antiques—and fighting monsters along the way! Their life was way more exciting than what I was hoping mine would now become. With the evil vanquished, I was ready for normal. Lots of it too! I couldn't think of anything more appealing!

"Wicked. I swear cat. You are trying my patience. Go put that back, this instant!"

Wicked had something small and grey in her mouth, and since she'd been stealing my socks lately, I already knew what she was bring me—or so I thought.

"Put that down or...*gah!*"

Wicked put it down all right, and it turned out to be a mouse. A very live mouse that scrambled away from the jaws of death, ran over my foot in the process and proceeded to run under the refrigerator where my feline giving pursuit manage to pounce—a moment too late.

The mouse was safe, and I was shrieking mess.

That's how my fiancé, Lorcan, found me when he rushed through the door convinced someone had broken in and was attempting murder. He even had a baseball bat in his hands looking ready to swing it and anyone and everyone causing me such distress.

I hurriedly pointed to the refrigerator and screamed again.

"You want me to beat the cat? What has Wicked done now?" he asked.

"Not the cat—well OK, maybe the cat for doing this to me today—but no, under the refrigerator. It's a mouse!" I explained.

Lorcan gave me such a look of incredulity it knocked me out of my panic and calmed me down so my breathing returned to normal.

"You just battled a year's worth of evil and a tiny mouse has you sounding like a banshee? Really?"

Lorcan had a point.

"It had glowing eyes? It might be a tiny malicious

demon mouse?" I tried to come up with anything at the spur of the moment to make an excuse for my irrational behavior, but we both knew I just failed my test as the newest dark witch to ever grace the town of Sweet Briar, Georgia. I was ashamed. What could make this moment worse?

"Did someone get murdered in here? What's all the fuss about?"

Oh yes. Things could definitely get worse.

I looked up to see Tiffany Clarkson, of the Sweet Briar Clarksons walking into my kitchen from the mudroom, holding her infernal rabbit, Lucifer, in her arms.

Tracking my yes to Lorcan, I went from nonsensical 'fraidy cat, to pissed off dark witch in five seconds flat.

Why was Lorcan with Tiffany, and what's more—why did he feel the need to bring her, and that darned rabbit, into my home?

Lorcan had some *splaining* to do—but quick!

SOCIAL MEDIA LINKS

"Coffee? Check. Pastries? Check. Fresh flowers? Che...hey! Wicked! Stop chewing on that arrangement, you demented furball. Get off the table!"

The last thing I needed today was a surly cat causing trouble and even one speck of anything out of place. Today was a very special day. Today both of my parents were coming home!

The old adage—*be careful what you wish for*—was running through my head as I looked out my kitchen window for the hundredth time this morning. You see, I am awaiting the return of my father, Charlie, and mom, Adelaide, from a hospital-like retreat they'd been away at for the last two weeks to try and have the witch clerics figure out what tracings of dark magic might still be swirling around inside my dad.

Our meeting had been bittersweet. I'd vanquished the evil Deanna Fredricks and the act of picking up the poppet had transported Charlie to my backyard and waiting family and friends, the most important of all being Adelaide—his long, lost love.

I missed witnessing their reunion because, yeah—battling an evil asshat of a witch!

My cousin Andrea said my two parents seeing each other for the first time in twenty-one years was the stuff of fairytales. But they didn't quite get their happily ever after as of yet. My father instantly began having dark magic withdrawals and despite him greeting me when I crossed back to where everyone was waiting for me to return, he'd become weakened and nauseous—so the paramedics were called.

My last image of the man had been his wild-eyed look and he was strapped to the gurney and a withered hand reaching for my mom. They had called from the hospital that he was being transferred to a witch's retreat, part spa part mental hospital where the foulest of magic could safely be expunged at the hands of some highly talented physicians in our magical world.

So, two long weeks of waiting had gone by, and now Charlie Sweet was finally coming home.

Those weeks would have been intolerable had my cousin's Maggie and Ellie Fortune not come down from North Carolina with their antique caravan. Although, with a murder happening and a psychotic stalker to deal with who decided Maggie would be his at all costs, things hadn't been as relaxing and fun as we'd hoped. At least it got my mind off my parents!

I promised my cousins that I'd head up to Mystic Valley, where they lived, when they were back at their family compound and not traveling all over the US selling and appraising antiques—and fighting monsters along the way! Their life was way more exciting than what I was hoping mine would now become. With the evil vanquished, I was ready for normal. Lots of it too! I couldn't think of anything more appealing!

"Wicked. I swear cat. You are trying my patience. Go put that back, this instant!"

Wicked had something small and grey in her mouth, and since she'd been stealing my socks lately, I already knew what she was bring me—or so I thought.

"Put that down or...*gah!*"

Wicked put it down all right, and it turned out to be a mouse. A very live mouse that scrambled away from the jaws of death, ran over my foot in the process and proceeded to run under the refrigerator where my feline giving pursuit manage to pounce—a moment too late.

The mouse was safe, and I was shrieking mess.

That's how my fiancé, Lorcan, found me when he rushed through the door convinced someone had broken in and was attempting murder. He even had a baseball bat in his hands looking ready to swing it and anyone and everyone causing me such distress.

I hurriedly pointed to the refrigerator and screamed again.

"You want me to beat the cat? What has Wicked done now?" he asked.

"Not the cat—well OK, maybe the cat for doing this to me today—but no, under the refrigerator. It's a mouse!" I explained.

Lorcan gave me such a look of incredulity it knocked me out of my panic and calmed me down so my breathing returned to normal.

"You just battled a year's worth of evil and a tiny mouse has you sounding like a banshee? Really?"

Lorcan had a point.

"It had glowing eyes? It might be a tiny malicious demon mouse?" I tried to come up with anything at the spur of the moment to make an excuse for my irrational behavior, but we both knew I just failed my test as the newest dark witch to ever grace the town of Sweet Briar, Georgia. I was ashamed. What could make this moment worse?

"Did someone get murdered in here? What's all the fuss about?"

Oh yes. Things could definitely get worse.

I looked up to see Tiffany Clarkson, of the Sweet Briar Clarksons walking into my kitchen from the mudroom, holding her infernal rabbit, Lucifer, in her arms.

Tracking my yes to Lorcan, I went from nonsensical 'fraidy cat, to pissed off dark witch in five seconds flat.

Why was Lorcan with Tiffany, and what's more—why did he feel the need to bring her, and that darned rabbit, into my home?

Lorcan had some *splaining* to do—but quick!

❧

I write in my own style that may not be everyone's cup of tea—so if you enjoy my characters and humor, my plots, how the storyline is developing, etc. and are eagerly anticipating the next in the series, be aware that I am just as excited as you are—I've found someone who thinks my story ideas are neat! That is thrilling for any writer to know (or it should be). THANK YOU!

Visit my official website to receive updates, find out about special offers and new releases, or read my blog about writing and farm life - complete with photos - you might even catch me mowing my ten acres (seriously): http://www.bettinamjohnson.net

For more information or to contact me:
author@bettinamjohnson.net

For even more (if you just can't enough of me) follow my Social Media Links

Mailing List - https://bit.ly/2BvQXmP
BookBub - https://bit.ly/2Epejwj
Goodreads - https://bit.ly/3aTejQW
Author Page - Amazon - https://amzn.to/3lj7L2L
Instagram - https://bit.ly/2QpZa01

TikTok - https://bit.ly/2PQa6Hg

MeWe - https://bit.ly/36A2RcM

Facebook - https://bit.ly/3gOaFZY

Twitter: https://bit.ly/3jahMgY
YouTube - https://bit.ly/2Stvy2X

ABOUT THE AUTHOR

I always knew I wanted to write. As a kid, way before the technology age had hit, I'd be stuck in the car with the folks as we drove from our home on Staten Island, NY, where I was born and raised, to our family property in the Catskill Mountains. To drive away boredom, I would sit, staring out the window, and create adventures of daring thieves riding horseback along the road, trying to escape the law. Other times I'd imagine a wild girl riding her unicorn into battle (I had a vivid imagination - we didn't have video games yet!).

As the years passed, I'd start writing a book, then stop, then start again only to let life get in the way, until one day I had an epiphany—a kick in the pants moment. If I waited any longer, all those wonderful characters in my head would never have their stories told, and that made me sad. So, I treated writing as my career. Once I started, it became apparent nothing would ever stop me again. YOU, dear reader, are stuck with me until I go off to that great library in the sky...or wherever writers go when they crumble to dust in front of their typewriters (or laptops...whatever!).

I live in the North Georgia mountains on what I like to call a farm, with my husband and almost adult kids, a Cairn Terrier, a bunch of cats, and fish. Occasionally other critters show up to keep things exciting.

BOOKS BY BETTINA M. JOHNSON

The Lily Sweet Mysteries:

Home Sweet Witch

Witch Way is Up?

How To Train Your Witch

Sweet Home Liliana

Witch Way Did He Go?

Revenge is Sweet, Witch

Witch and Peace

The Sweet Spell of Success

I Spell Trouble (Coming soon)

Sweet Briar Witch (Coming soon)

The Fortune-Telling Twins Mysteries:

A Tale of Two Sisters

Double Toil and Trouble

Fire and Earth, Sisters at Birth

Kindred Spirits (Coming soon)

A Djinn and Tonic (Coming soon)

www.ingramcontent.com/pod-product-compliance
Lightning Source LLC
LaVergne TN
LVHW090949080826
845145LV00003B/941

* 9 7 8 1 7 3 6 5 1 7 6 2 8 *